Deepak Pyakurel

THE WAVE OF LIFE

DORRANCE
PUBLISHING CO
EST. 1920
PITTSBURGH, PENNSYLVANIA 15238

Dorrance Publishing Co
585 Alpha Drive
Pittsburgh, PA 15238
Visit our website at *www.dorrancebookstore.com*

ISBN: 978-1-6853-7151-7
eISBN: 978-1-6853-7994-0

THE WAVE OF LIFE

1

"Fuck! This damn life!" He cursed himself.

He seemed to be very bored with life or he had made a big mistake in life that he would regret for the rest of his life. Or, in the experience of life, the weeds of disgust had grown innumerable in his heart.

He, namely Rajendra Khadka, former colonel of the Nepal Army, then Royal Nepal Army! He is currently driving around New York's busy city, Jackson Heights to find a parking lot. The common problem on this busy road is the lack of parking space. Suppose, finding a parking lot is like winning a small battle!

After driving around for half an hour, he finally found a parking lot on a street a short distance from his apartment. He breathed a sigh of relief. He stopped the engine of the car. He looked at the time on his mobile. It was six o'clock. He thought to himself, *it's not time to go home.*

Of course, he usually drives until nine or ten o'clock at night. He is a driver by profession in the United States. Let's say he's a taxi driver. In fact, the yellow or green cab here is only called a taxi, but not the kind of taxi he drives. In colloquial language, the vehicle he drives here is called Uber. The job is the same to carry passengers.

But it is not like picking up a passenger by taking a detour like a taxi. All you have to do is use the app of the company that facilitates the transport and the message will come that there is a passenger nearby. No orders, just information!

In other words, after receiving information about the theft, the police should run after the thief, even if all the work is left unfinished. However, Uber drivers do not have such a compulsion. If you like to pick up that customer, pick it up, otherwise you don't care!

If he picked up the passenger, he would get money. That is a different matter. Let's say, 'He is his own master, he is his own servant!'

In the beginning, he used to rent a car and drive it. Now he has his own car. Rent is also saved. It is also used to move the family around. It has also become easier for him to buy household items. For him, it has become a money-making machine. What fun!

In New York, the ultimate goal of most Nepalis is to end their career in driving!

Most Nepalis are attracted to this driving profession, in terms of income, maybe! Then, again, your freedom will not be in the hands of others. If you like, you can drive, if you don't like, you can rest.

As soon as you wake up in the morning, if you wish you can go to work, otherwise you can start driving from noon to late at night. If you have a good income today, if you wish you can go home in the evening. If not, you can go to Jackson Heights and drink alcohol at the Nepali kitchen.

Even if Nepali kitchen doesn't serve alcohol there, you can bring it from outside and drink it. You may meet some Nepalis you know there. Even if you don't meet any acquaintances, you can chat with the sisters who work there.

Memories of Nepal, memories of relatives can be forgotten to some extent in Jackson Heights. It seems that Jackson Heights is the common ground for Nepalis living in New York. Suppose a piece of Nepal! Mini Nepal! We do not know what other Nepalis think. But former

Colonel Rajendra Khadka feels the same way in Jackson Heights. He would occasionally say to his friends, "If it weren't for Jackson

Heights, I would have returned to Nepal right away. Anyway, Jackson Heights has kept me going. Jackson Heights has

softened my heart many times when I am moved by the memory of Nepal."

He thought, *I haven't been to the Nepali kitchen for a long time. It is finally six o'clock. Wife will not come home before nine o'clock. Why stay alone at home in the evening? Instead, it would be better to go to the Nepali kitchen and drink.*

The colonel's footsteps hurried to Jackson Heights and his compelled shadow trailed behind him!

2

He entered the liquor store before entering the Nepali kitchen. He looked at the rack decorated with whiskey. The colonel thought to himself, *a quarter is not enough, half a bottle is fine! If there is someone I know in the restaurant, then a quarter will not be enough. Instead, I buy half a bottle and take it home if I can't drink it completely.*

Carrying half a bottle of whiskey, he entered the kitchen. He went straight to the basement. And he looked around to see if there was an empty table.

"Oh, Colonel!" A familiar voice caught his attention. He was a former SP of Nepal Police, drinking alone. The colonel knew him from Nepal.

"You too? Isn't it your duty today? I haven't seen you for a long time? Are you busy making money or what?" The colonel fired a barrage of questions, adding a little sarcasm to his surprise.

The SP also said with a smile on his face, "You always enjoy life. We also like to have fun sometimes in life, don't we? Colonel!"

The colonel thought for a moment. *Is he making fun of me or is he pouring out old rage?* The colonel thought, *Why spoil the atmosphere by arguing unnecessarily?* Then he asked the SP, "Well, I'm alone, you're drinking alone. Should I sit at your table, sir?"

"Did you tease or ask me? Do we have to go through such a formality?" The SP looked sad, "Should we renew our old identity from time to time?" He became very emotional.

Maybe SP seems to be intoxicated now or he may have been nostalgic for the old days, the colonel speculated.

Both of them locked the sarcasm and jokes in their hearts and hugged each other. And they both cheered the rest of the whiskey in the bottle that the SP had. It was still a long night to cheer for the bottle brought by the colonel.

Both remained silent for a while, a thoughtful silence! Such silence is like when we were planning to bury the body after the murder!

"Why are you still working as a security guard? That too at night duty!" The colonel broke the silence, "Run Uber instead! Be your own master, be your own servant!"

After thinking for a while, the SP replied, "I don't like to drive. While driving, you don't have time to eat or sleep. Other than that, there is a big problem with toilets. So much in America, even in New York! Big problem with toilets! Where to park? Where to go to the toilet? If you go to the restaurant for the toilet, first you have to buy something, you have to pay money. Until then, that's fine! But you also have to find a place to park! It's like winning the lottery! And how long do we stop urinating? Again, stopping urination also affects the kidneys. Some even urinate in a bottle inside the car! Don't you have to look for a place to throw the bottle again?"

The SP took a deep breath, as if he were the main victim!

"Fuck! Big talk! He who has no experience is the one who talks more!"

The colonel said to himself, did not object to the SP.

Both became silent. The SP swallowed the rest of the liquor at once. The colonel took a small sip.

The colonel looked around. Almost all the tables were packed. Some were eating Nepali food. A group of women were eating bread, vegetables, pickles, potatoes, talking loudly about someone else. Some were eating Tibetan food. Four or five boys were drinking beer with a set of
typical Newari food.

The atmosphere in the restaurant was growing, the noise was increasing.

It was as if the colonel was not in New York City, but he was sitting in a dark restaurant on the streets of Kathmandu, drinking local liquor!

After enjoying the atmosphere here, the colonel often returned to his youth in the same way as he sometimes returned home on vacation.

"Aren't you in a hurry, no? Tomorrow and the day after tomorrow you will be on holiday! Is everyone in the family okay? Do your children work or not? Do they go to college too? Children's education should be continued, but it doesn't matter if they don't work. If they don't have an American degree, they have to work as hard as we do. Even if we bring a PhD certificate from Nepal, the work we do is of a low standard," the colonel said, not to the SP, but to himself like a cannabis addict.

The SP did not respond. Instead, he kept shaking his head in unison, like the pendulum of a clock hanging on the wall!

The more beer bottles were opened, the louder the boys' voices became. Meanwhile, the voices of the colonel and the SP were fading. Instead, the boys' voices caught their attention.

"Fuck! I didn't earn much this weekend. Yesterday I was drunk, I didn't even touch the car. Nothing happened today. This week I can't even pay the rent! Look, I'll run from morning to night tomorrow! Dude! you have your own car, you don't have to worry about the rent!" He expressed his grief.

"No, man! You were able to enter the United States in three million rupees. But I paid five million rupees. That much money! A lot of loan money, that too at a high interest rate! How can I pay the debt if I don't drive for fourteen or fifteen hours a day? You came to America after selling

the land, you don't have any debt," said another one, taking the pain out of his heart like someone drying the green corn in the yard!

Suppose sorrow, pain, problems, grievances take up a lot of space in the heart, then happiness and enthusiasm will not find a place to live!

Both the colonel and the SP have understood that these boys are also Uber drivers. The SP smiled invisibly. Earlier, the colonel's question and the answer he gave seemed to be meaningful!

But, the colonel became thoughtful. Moreover, he felt puffy in front of the SP!

"Damn! Anyone who drives Uber, even those who come to America by crossing the river, even those who come to America by plane. Even if they do dish-washing in the beginning, the ultimate goal is the driver! Whether you pass only eight classes or do double MA, the work is the same! Fuck! Life!" He cursed himself first.

Then, the colonel suddenly vomited the hatred that had been lingering in the well of his mind for years, "Fucking Maoists!"

The colonel no longer wanted to stay there. He felt ashamed along with the fear that his old identity and position would be exposed in front of everyone. He swallowed the remaining whiskey in a glass. Leaving the rest of the bottle of liquor to SP, he climbed the ladder to the counter.

When he reached home, his wife had not arrived. He looked at his watch. It was finally nine o'clock. He thought his wife would not arrive before half past nine. *Plus, today is the weekend. Even so, the train runs late on weekends!* He thought. He does not like to be alone at home. That is why he used to leave late in the morning and return home late at night.

The colonel thought, *I'll drink a peg or two. The previous drinks have no effect on me now. I don't know when my wife will come home!*

Thinking this, the colonel jumped up from his seat and took out a whiskey from the cupboard and poured a nice peg into the glass and put two pieces of ice cube too. He shook the glass hard, as if to melt the ice and make water immediately. He drank half of the liquor and lay down on the sofa.

"Is this life?" He asked himself a question.

The answer did not break the silence. Perhaps, the answer itself has been immersed in years of penance in the remote cave of the mind!

The mobile phone rang. He picked up the phone. His wife asked him, "Where are you? At work or at home?"

"I'm at home. I didn't have much work today so I came home early. Are you coming?" The colonel inquired.

"I'm coming. It'll take about half an hour. The train is running late today."

The call was interrupted as the wife could not say much. *Maybe the network inside the train is broken,* he thought.

The sound of shoes on the ladder distracted him. He found out that it was his wife's walk.

For more than twenty-five years, he has stretched out his marriage and brought it here. There were ups and downs, joys and sorrows, love and grievances, twists and turns, but the flood of time did not break the bond so easily!

"I have got no good tips today. Business is also very slow. When will this winter end? Customers also come only for eye-brows. Such customers don't give us much tips. Salary alone is not enough for us! The greed for tips is more like the love of interest than the love of capital. And how much did you earn today?"

He had become accustomed to his wife's grumbling. He had developed the habit of listening rather than answering questions. When no answer came from her husband, she went into the room and changed her clothes.

"Don't you want to eat? I'll check what's left in the fridge, lentils, vegetables, and meat. I'm not in the mood to cook today. I'll eat whatever I have. How much do you like to eat?"

He was used to his wife's lazy habit after coming home from work.

"Okay. I sat in the restaurant for a while. I had some snacks. I have enough. I'm not really hungry," he said to his wife. "What time does our daughter come today? It's probably a little late on the weekends. Our son is probably having fun with his friends. He doesn't do anything; he doesn't pay attention to his studies. Our daughter also goes to college and works in a restaurant. You spoiled the son!" The colonel expressed his anger in front of his wife.

"Where did I spoil my son? He is old enough to have fun! In old age, you still have fun with friends. What is possible by talking about your youth? Remember for a moment what you did in the past?" His wife retaliated by attacking him.

Suppose, she hid the arrow of words with care for years and waited for the opportunity to

use it in the right place!

He thought it would be a loss to stretch the conversation, and to close the chapter, he said, "OK, let's eat now. I'm asleep too. I have to get to work early tomorrow morning."

Alcoholism worked well! After lying on the bed, the colonel started snoring. The wife became busy on Facebook.

4

The colonel woke up early in the morning. What to do even after getting up? He thought and was lying on the bed. His wife was fast asleep. He also got up and lay down on the bed feeling lazy to make tea.

Even though his body was in the United States, his mind was mostly in Nepal. The magnet that attracts his mind is still in Nepal! In any case, the important age of his life was spent in Nepal. What a pleasure it was to see a fifty-story skyscraper! For him, the moments spent in different districts were the invaluable treasure of life, which he used to pull out of the box of his mind and become nostalgic from time to time.

He spent most of his life in the barracks rather than at home. He preferred the remote district to his nearest job.

He never agreed with the popular belief that 'childhood is the golden moment of life!', but the days of his youth were more dear to him.

Like almost everyone else, his childhood was a simple one. Swimming in the river, running away from school to go to the cinema, throwing books after returning from school and running to play football and volleyball. He used to eat what he found at lunch and run to play. Homework? At that time, who knew what the name of the animal was homework? The next day, everyone had to show the teacher what he had written. English seemed the most difficult for him. Even the teacher found it difficult to teach him. Then math and science seemed difficult to him.

Even if you could do everything else, where was the time to study? As soon as he started eating rice due to the tiredness of school and evening sports during the day, sleep would start calling him to bed. He would always swear that he would get up early in the morning and do his homework, and then he went to bed. Sleep was already waiting for him!

He woke up in the morning feeling lazy. Today would have been a holiday, a stranger at school would have died! He used to spend the mornings thinking like this. He could not read or write even in the morning! Even if he made many excuses to other teachers for not being able to complete the school lesson of the previous day, how could he avoid the beating of Ghising Sir? He would instead hit the duster in his hand, but would punch him in the mouth with his fist. That angry Darjeeling sir!

Suppose he was frightened, as if he were about to be beaten again. He smiled, remembering that the fear was still in his mind.

He used to enjoy swimming in the river the most. In the summer months, he would return from school at eleven o'clock in the morning. He ate, and headed straight for the river. And all day swimming, fishing, cooking, eating! All day long he lived by the river. Why did he have to read and write? What tense of tomorrow! Tension was about how to raise money to watch a movie in the cinema hall, even if it was stolen. Otherwise, the school had asked for money to donate. He even lied at home saying that he would be beaten by the headmaster if he did not donate.

He had never been indifferent to his childhood activities like playing Marbles during school holidays, playing Dandibio, playing cards, flying kites, waiting for festivals for long holidays, enjoying Dashain and Tihar. He was active in all activities.

Forty or fifty years ago, almost everyone's childhood was spent in the same way. Fun life! Tension free! No worries for tomorrow!

However, if someone failed in class, he would be ashamed to be in front of his friends. Everyone teased him. He was also beaten at home. Old friends would leave him. So, even if he

didn't read at other times, he used to read with interest a week before the exam started. He used to make a routine and stick it on the wall of the bedroom to decide which subjects to study at which time. Even if he failed in one or two subjects, he would have climbed one class.

He did not have to repeat it in any class. He climbed one class after another. That was his greatest achievement. He was also exempted from doing household chores. That did not apply to his siblings, as they were repeated in the same class from time to time.

The days of childhood and adolescence passed like that, without any worries. Of course, reading was just a matter of concern. That was a compelling concern. The rest of the worries were carried on the shoulders of father and mother!

Anyway, he managed to pass the SLC (School Leaving Certificate) in the third division. Passing was a big thing then. Only two or three people from schools across the district brought First Division at that time.

His respect among his family and relatives suddenly increased, as the stream near the farm grew in the rain!

Now he considered himself mature. He felt that he had grown up and was responsible. And he also reassured the mind that he should do something in life now.

"What are you already thinking? Do you have any tension?"

At the sound of his wife's voice, he inadvertently braked in his past life, just as a speeding driver brakes when he suddenly sees a large hole in the road. He had to land the flight of the past in the present.

"No, there is no such thing. My eyes opened quickly, then I couldn't sleep. And I remembered Nepal," he said, "I will make tea and bring it." He got up and went to the kitchen.

He knew that his wife was too lazy to get up in the morning to make tea, and his wife would say to him from time to time, "The taste of the tea you make is different. What I make is always junk! If the tea I drink in the morning is not tasty, my mood will deteriorate throughout the day."

5

He was upset today. A thick cloud of sadness hovered in his mind. His wife left for work in the morning after having tea and breakfast. The daughter was sleeping. He did not know when his son came to sleep at night. He hadn't woken up yet, maybe he's sleeping. And even the colonel didn't feel like going to work today.

How much work to do in life? Why bother so much? His mind said. The son and daughter are also studying, earning some money. My wife earns well too. There is no need to send money to anyone in Nepal, there is no mother or father. The brothers have their own family, their own world. Everyone is fine. I don't have to help. They have not even asked for help. And what about plowing like an ox for ten or twelve hours a day! He sighed for a long time.

Suddenly he took a bottle of whiskey out of the cupboard. Yesterday's hang was still holding him. He put a big peg in the glass. Maybe in the morning he didn't put the ice-cube, but he did put in some water. He drank about half the whiskey at once. And he hid the glass under the sofa, so that the children would not see the bottle if they woke up.

If no one says 'you did a good job!' when you drink alcohol in the morning, the family members feel even worse!

The intoxication slowly began to rise, but he began to decline in the past.

After passing SLC, he joined the arts faculty in the college, feeling that it would be easier to pass. Again, he still did not have a good friendship with study! He just had to pass. Anyway he was ready to cheat in the exam. And he knew how to write on his own copy exactly what the person on the bench next to him wrote!

He put more emphasis on sports than on studies, thinking that some of his relatives were policemen and others were in the army. For a cadet, a diploma pass certificate would have been enough, but the body had to be strong. However, he did not neglect his studies. If he didn't have a certificate, he wouldn't get a job just by showing a strong body. Putting both things in balance, he moved forward. Anyway, the dream had to come true!

"Have you been drinking? Why are you so serious?" The colonel was suddenly startled by his daughter's voice.

Embarrassed like a criminal caught red-handed stealing, he asked his daughter, "Shall I make breakfast ready?" He was more afraid of his daughter than his wife when it came to alcohol.

"After a while. First, I'll be fresh. My brother will get up too, and we'll eat together," said the daughter and went into the bathroom.

On this occasion, he took out a glass from under the sofa and swallowed the remaining liquor. And he let out a long sigh, "Fuck! This is a disgusting life!" He muttered.

Taking the opportunity of his daughter taking a bath and his son sleeping, he put on another peg. He took a small sip. And soon after, his son woke up.

"What time did you come yesterday? You must have come drunk, haven't you?" He interrogated his son just as the police interrogated the thief.

"I came around twelve o'clock. I had a light drink with my friends, not much," said the son, as if he had opened his heart to his friend, not to his father.

He said nothing. Instead, he started thinking about it. *This is America! Own your own life after becoming an adult! No one's rights in his life, no obligation to anyone!*

This is America! He laughed thoughtfully, a sarcastic smile to himself! Not to his daughter, not to his son, not to his wife! That smile towards the helplessness of one's own life! Towards an invisible game played by time sitting behind the scenes! To the compulsion of the opposing player who has no choice but to watch the clumsy player score dozens of goals in ninety minutes without a goalkeeper!

6

Colonel Rajendra Khadka set aside all his time for himself today. He didn't go to work, he took full rest. He cooked food, cooked mutton. He also made his favorite tomato pickle.

He also drank alcohol from time to time without letting the children know. Today he presented himself in a festive mood! He left himself free, he did not listen to his heart and mind. Needless to say, he didn't pay attention to anything else.

After eating, the children left the house. He did not know where his son had gone. The daughter, of course, went to work. He was in a dilemma whether to use a laptop or watch a movie on TV. He had read the news about Nepal online in the morning. Instead, he decided to watch a new movie on Netflix.

And he started watching the recently released Hindi film. He also drank a little alcohol. While watching the movie, he felt dizzy. He turned off the TV and went to bed, And soon he fell asleep.

He woke up. He looked at the time on his mobile. It's five o'clock. *I have slept a lot. What to do now? How much alcohol to drink at home again? It would be better to go to Jackson Heights now!* He thought to himself.

He changed his clothes and left the house. And he took a quick step towards the Nepali kitchen. Suppose, if he arrives late, he finds that all the food in the Nepali kitchen is empty like in a wedding party!

The colonel bought liquor from the liquor store and entered the Nepali kitchen. Of course, there are other Nepali restaurants around, but he finds this restaurant comfortable.

He saw Pasang, who was always drunk, sitting alone in the corner drinking and he also went to the table where Pasang was sitting.

"Oh, Colonel! After a long time, I finally saw you today," Pasang said sarcastically.

The alcohol seems to have reached the top of his head, the colonel thought. But he said nothing. The colonel sat down at the table next to Pasang.

"Just recently or since noon?" That's all the colonel asked.

"Three o'clock. It's been three hours. I drank a lot. Did you bring a bottle?" Pasang glanced at the plastic bag the colonel was carrying.

"I brought half a bottle," said the colonel, and poured a large peg into his glass. There was about half the alcohol left in Pasang's glass.

The colonel asked, "Do you add this drink after you finish it or do you add a drink to it?"

"Okay, let's add to that," Pasang said hurriedly.

Maybe that's what Pasang thought. Before his glass is empty, the colonel can drink the whole bottle, or if an acquaintance comes, he can drink the rest! Also, if the colonel gets an urgent call, he can have a quick drink and leave immediately!

Pasang has nothing to do with the brand, nor with the breed of liquor. Whether it's whiskey or vodka, rum or brandy, it's all about drinking! All he knows is that the caste or religion of alcohol is to get drunk, no matter what alcohol he drinks!

Pasang pretends not to have to drink beer! But it was not always as he thought. Sometimes, he did not know that he had finished drinking the liquor he had taken home. And there was a problem! The liquor store next to his house would have been closed at eleven o'clock at night, only to be reopened at eleven o'clock the next morning.

It is at this time that he used to take refuge in beer! And he would go to the small store.

Like a grocery store in Nepal where you can find almost everything you need for your home. Wake up 24 hours a day! There is no alcohol, but there are different types of beer. It's as if special representatives of beer from around the world have gathered in one place to sit down for a meeting!

The colonel likes to drink with Pasang. Even though Pasang is a drunkard, he never keeps sin in his mind, he expresses his thoughts clearly. He does not hide anything from family relationships to his external intimate relationships. He says everything openly. He doesn't care what others think or say.

Pasang has been in the United States for more than twenty years. He has been an American citizen for more than ten years. He has been married twice so far. Both women were abandoned by their husbands. As interest was added to the capital, he had to embrace their children first, otherwise he would have to abandon his wives. He was willing to bear the brunt of interest, but he could not give up capital! After taking a loan, the interest will automatically follow!

The son and daughter born to his first wife and her first husband are still in Nepal. The daughter is married in a good family and has a comfortable life. The son's business is also good. And he doesn't have to worry about his eldest wife! He has already passed the four storied house in his wife's name and is now living in the United States with his youngest wife. He doesn't have to worry about them, they don't worry about him either!

In the end, the contract to take care of him fell on his younger wife! It is as if the parents lovingly gave the daughter a dowry out of the entire share of the son!

He was still confused as to why he had fled to the United States. Everything was in Nepal. She was a loving wife. The children were also wise and loving. He had everything in Nepal. The eldest wife still loves him because he gave her great support in times of grief, even though he lived with the youngest.

"Even though I left her, the eldest wife did not look for another man, but raised the children well." Pasang used to praise his eldest wife in the Nepali kitchen from time to time, whether he knew someone in front of him or not. Who cares!

Disappointed, he entered the United States. He had a habit of living abroad. Two years before coming to the United States, he returned to Nepal after living in Japan for seven years. He bought a house in Kathmandu with the money he earned in Japan.

He was alone. And he was cool too!

He started drinking at a local restaurant near his house. The owner of the restaurant was very beautiful. When he started drinking, he gradually fell in love with the woman.

He did not look left or right when he heard the story of a woman who was completely ignored by her husband by bringing a young wife and seeing the sad faces of the children. He did not ask anyone. Parents were already gone, so no need to ask! He did not consider it necessary to ask the brothers. He didn't care about his relatives.

Witnessing some friends, he went to the monastery and made the owner of a local restaurant the owner of his own life. And he also shouldered the entire responsibility of the children he got for free!

Colonel and Pasang cheered again. And the both seemed in a good mood.

"Coming to the United States and bringing a Tibetan wife was the biggest mistake of my life," Pasang said seriously. And he suddenly looked worried, "I can't leave my current wife, I can't bring another one too. I'm sixty years old, Colonel Saab!"

Pasang took a sip and said, "The only daughter I have ever had is from my youngest wife. I love her very much, probably because of my own blood. She is eighteen, studying to be a nurse. I'm not worried about her future."

Suddenly, he shouted, "I brought her spoiled son to America anyway. I thought he would do something when he was brought to America, but he started smoking marijuana instead! He doesn't work, nor does he speak well to me. Mother's lovely son! If I shouted at her son a little louder, I would have a fight with her. I don't have to say anything to him! 'I can leave my husband, but I can't leave my son. I don't even tell my son to leave home. Whether my son works or not, I can earn and raise my son. Others don't have to worry,' she says when she gets angry and our conversation stops for months. Thankfully, she cooks the food and keeps it for me!"

Pasang did not speak for a while. Well, what did he play in his mind? And sipping a glass of drink, he became serious and said, "When my daughter reaches the age of eighteen, I will ask for a divorce from my younger wife. And, sometimes, I feel like going to live with my eldest wife in Nepal."

"Even when I am living here with my youngest wife, the eldest did not go with the other. One mind says, if I go back after so many years, would the eldest wife give me a warm welcome? Wouldn't she hit me with an arrow of heartbreaking words? Another mind says, when you support a person who is in distress, he will support you in any situation when you are in trouble! It's as if my own mind is sitting in the corner and weighing me!" Pasang stopped talking.

Suppose, he thought that the conversation turned to the other side. Let's say that a person walking at his own pace thinking of a highway suddenly stopped when he saw the subway!

Pasang remembered something, and then he started again, "I stayed with my eldest wife for two whole months when I went to Nepal last year. We went to Pokhara, Lumbini, Sauraha altogether. It was fun. However, the elder used to sprinkle chili powder on the sour wound from time to time as if she had tasted the salt in the vegetables. 'It seems like the youngest loves you so much! You used to be so thin, now you are fat! Why do you pretend to love me? Believe what the eye sees rather than what the ear hears!"

Without saying a word, Pasang poured alcohol from the bottle into the glass. A little water was added. He didn't even ask the colonel to add alcohol. Maybe Pasang's consciousness was under the influence of alcohol!

Pasang drank again. And he slammed the glass on the table. Suppose it was necessary to inform everyone present in the restaurant that he was very drunk!

"Should I go to Nepal or stay here? I am in a dilemma. There are still four or five years left to get retired benefits. I don't get along with my wife and her son here. Even if we live under one roof, it is as if we live hundreds of miles away. No dialogue, no formality!" The colonel did not know that Pasang was thinking so deeply. Perhaps bitter experiences and sadness that make a person mature!

Pasang added alcohol. The colonel did not stop Pasang, realizing the inner conflict within him.

After sipping half the liquor, he started again, "How can I go to show my face to the eldest after spending twenty years with the youngest, as if I have only my own selfish interests. For all those years, I did not care for the eldest. I was satisfied that I had given financial security to the eldest. When you don't have anything, even if you get little, it becomes a very big thing. But, when people get that, they feel the lack of other things again!"

Pasang was confused for a while. He rolled his eyes to see if there was alcohol in the glass. He was relieved to see half the alcohol left. He did not rush to clear the glass of alcohol.

As the skilled narrator rested in the middle and did not move an inch, he started narrating in the same rhythm and speed again, "What to do in Nepal at this age? How long will the money saved here be spent in Nepal? And again, there is no question of claiming the money coming from the rent of the eldest house, nor of extending a hand in front of the children. So I have thought of making an allowance by staying here for three or four years, I have paid taxes for so many years! The allowance will also be one thousand and two hundred per month. If you get that much money, life will be comfortable in Nepal, right? Even though the house is now in the name of the eldest wife, I bought it with my own money. Even if the eldest doesn't do anything else, I hope she gives me a room to sleep in!"

Pasang made his future plans in this way, as if life should go smoothly according to his plan. Suppose, life is like a movie written by a script writer to make a fictional story come true!

Pasang calmed down and picked up the glass from the table. He did not completely empty the alcohol, leaving about half left. Maybe he was relieved when he opened his heart! So he did not rush to drink alcohol.

The colonel also took a sip and got lost in his own world for a while.

"Is the alcohol over or left?"

The colonel was startled by Pasang's sharp voice, like a man who is deep asleep when someone comes close to his ear and blows his whistle loudly!

"It's over!" The colonel said in a low voice.

The colonel was not as drunk as Pasang. The colonel looked at his watch. It was ten

o'clock. He thought, *Now I have to walk. How much alcohol to drink, as always. I have to drink again tomorrow, even if I drink at home.*

And he went to the toilet because he felt a strong urge to urinate. When he came back from the toilet, he saw Pasang reaching the next table and cheering with others.

"This man will never get better. If he continues like this, he will soon be past himself before his dream is fulfilled!"

The colonel's heart sank.

Pasang has been drinking a lot, he is not conscious. Again, in front of everyone, 'Colonel Saab! Wouldn't you like a little drink? He can say.' The colonel thought that it would be better to walk without calling him now and he went straight to the ladder.

Some of his family, neighbors, relatives and kin were in the palace, in the police, in the army, so his attraction was the same. His mind was already drawn to the army's combat dress.

Even before passing the IA (Intermediate of Arts), he was already preparing for the second lieutenant. Most importantly, he emphasized physical exercise. Physical strength which was essential in the platoon rather than reading. If you could pass in Physical and Medical, then writing and interview was an internal matter. Inwardly, source and force would have worked. One of his family members was working at the palace. He also received reassurance and encouragement from him.

He was also busy with his studies. And he also passed IA at once. He did not care what percentage came in the result. Passing was a breath of satisfaction for him. The weapon needed for the second lieutenant fell into his hands. All that remained was to use the weapon!

He never hesitated to do hard physical exercises to make his dream come true. Some of them used to run away while training. At such times, he was happy that the competition was reduced. He was selected as a cadet due to his hard work and the support of his relatives.

And the day he received the second lieutenant's medal, he considered it the most unforgettable moment of his life. The rest was just the beginning!

Anyway, his life had found a way to move forward now. Walking on the journey of life is the beginning of the justification of living!

Just as everyone has big dreams in their minds, so did he! Who could stop him from dreaming of reaching a good position in one day?

After getting a job, another obligation was added to get married and settle down. At that time, the age of twenty-four or twenty-five was considered to be too late for marriage. Physically, he had received many internal signals. His family and relatives were already working hard to get him married. Everyone was in a hurry for his marriage.

At that time, being an army officer was a source of pride and dignity in the society. Well, even if it's not worth being proud of in terms of money. He didn't even need to give so much importance to money. Ancestral wealth was plentiful. He was able to cover his expenses from his salary. What were his other expenses? From time to time, he would gather his village friends and take them to a local restaurant for a drink and proudly praised the army!

In such gatherings, it was forbidden for anyone to talk about political issues under the influence of alcohol. He used to get very angry when someone tried to talk about politics by mistake under the influence of intoxication and then he would say, "You don't know anything! Don't talk too much! We are the true servants of the king! The king's true soldier! Our supreme commander is the king! We do not consider these ministers and the Prime Minister special! Do you understand?"

Everyone was aware of his stubborn and rude nature. No one wanted to argue with him. Everyone was wondering why they should take unnecessary risks and misunderstandings. And then they had to rely on him for alcohol too, because they were unemployed!

His thinking and the culture inherited from his dynasty were also traditional and feudal. Moreover, the schooling and training of the army pushed him to bigotry! There was a drought of modern thinking. The scope of his reading was limited. Far from reading books, he also found it annoying to read newspapers.

He used to say that magazines only write nonsense. He considered the briefings given by the bosses to be true. He did not think about life, nor did he worry about life. 'Whatever happens, enjoy it' was his life mantra!

After joining the army, there was a difference in food. Drinks were included in it. He used to drink with pleasure. Life in the barracks was cool too! He did not have much responsibility towards his family. In other words, he was not obliged to meet the needs of others.

One evening he was drinking alone in the canteen. The soldier came running and said, "Someone has called from your house. It's urgent!"

Who called at this time? Is there such an urgency? Thinking, he got up from his chair.

Taking the receiver of the phone to his ear, he was just about to say 'hello', his brother's voice from the other side said, "You come home tomorrow or the day after tomorrow anyway! There is talk of marriage from a good family. The girl is also beautiful and cultured. You should not lose her. You know, finding the right girl these days is like looking for corn in an empty field! Think for yourself! You know better than I do."

Without giving him a chance to speak, his brother hung up the phone.

In the calm lake of his mind, the talk of marriage sailed the boat. A sweet, thrilling wave rose in his mind. The imaginary form of the future wife was secretly drawn to his mind.

In the picture of his mind, he was shocked to see the form of the same young woman often seen in a dream, just like when a person returns from abroad after many years, he is shocked to see that the dirt road he used to walk on has turned into a smooth road!

8

He arranged for three or four days off to go home. He lied to the boss of the office that his father was sick at home. He did not say that he was going to see the bride. Probably, because of hesitation and shame! The girl he was looking to marry was a close relative of his family. And both families already knew each other and knew everything. He was meeting the girl for the first time. It was decided to introduce the boy and girl in the house of the girl's relative.

At first glance, his mind accepted the girl. He said to himself, Black Beauty!

At that time, it was not customary for a boy and a girl to sit and listen to each other in private. It was a great thing to see each other.

"Do you like the girl? Shall I make sure to get married?" Asked the brother.

His brother was the head of the family. The brother did not need to consult his parents about anything. What to say to his brother, he felt ashamed. He just shook his head in approval. His brother was happy, because his younger brother was marrying a girl who was related to his wife. At that time, it was not customary to ask a girl if she liked the boy.

Pandit also fixed the wedding day by looking at the calendar. At that time, the practice of engagement was not as strong as it is now.

Also, since there were family ties on both sides, it would not be dignified to have any doubts from the girl's side. In the end, the two sides agreed to have a grand wedding anyway.

The next day, he returned to the barracks. He felt it was right to show up for work. What was the use of sitting at home? He had no choice but to wait for the marriage to open his heart to the girl he was going to marry.

His mind also rejoiced in the barracks. He was accustomed to the services, hospitality and food of the barracks. He would remember his future wife from time to time, but not in a clear way. He would disappear into himself for a while with the same blurred face.

He didn't even have a number to call. He didn't even have to write a letter. If others found the letter, his own self-esteem would be hurt. On the contrary, he was ridiculed! Instead, the best solution was to wait for the wedding day. Imagination had its place, in which there was no obstruction or interruption.

Life in the barracks! He was having an affair with alcohol in the evening. Away from home, independent life! The fun of freedom is different! He enjoyed it. At times, he felt unhappy, thinking that his personal freedom would be curtailed after marriage. Then, he would swallow another peg, saying, "I will endure whatever happens!"

Time did not have to wait! Time was moving at its own pace, playing hide and seek with day and night!

As the wedding day approached, his mind became more and more excited. Again, fear shared the room with curiosity in his mind. 'Wouldn't the weight of new life crush me?' Fear frightened him from time to time.

Anyway, he had to drive the car of life. In any case, traveling with someone is more fun than traveling alone in the car of life! Physical needs are different!

Whether he read it or heard someone say it, he remembered, "Life is a combination of happiness and sorrow. Sometimes more, sometimes less, not the same!"

"What are you thinking seriously? It looks like you drank too much! Always the same routine? It's too much! And you never listen to me!" He was startled by his wife's hoarse voice.

He was forced to make a sudden landing on the current runway of an airplane he had been traveling on in the past. And He said, "There is no such thing. I used to know you had come from your walk on the ladder. But I was lost in thought today, I did not know you came."

He did not say that he was lost in her imagination in the old flash-back of twenty-five or twenty-six years ago. He didn't want to tell her, let's say!

He kept saying that it is better to keep a lot of things with oneself, while sharing with others there is a fear of losing its true sweetness!

9

He woke up early in the morning. It's seven o'clock. He knew it was too early to get up at seven in the United States. Those who go to work in the morning are different!

After finishing his daily routine in the bathroom, he made tea for himself and his wife. Children do not get up before eleven o'clock. They hang out on their mobile phones till two o'clock at night. It is a coincidence that everyone sits down to eat together. Everyone is busy in their own world! He thought so much while making tea.

After a light breakfast and tea, his wife hurried to work. He doesn't like the word 'hurry'. He is the master of his own mind. Absolutely cool! *The sooner you go to work, the more you earn, the later you go, the less you earn. Today I am leaving late, how hard it is to work now even in old age!* He thought to himself.

Again, he did not have to worry so much about money. He has been in the United States for more than eleven or twelve years. My wife also earns. The children have grown up now. They can earn on their own. Sooner or later, the son will start earning money, he reassured himself.

The sun is shining today. Now it is like going to a nearby park and doing light exercise, he made a plan.

When he reached the park, he jogged for a while. He also

practiced some of the easy exercises he did while in the army. He also started sweating lightly. He got tired quickly due to age. He sat on the bench and began to relax. And he began to spend time observing the environment and activities there.

Probably due to school vacation, many children were playing happily. Some of the little ones were playing ping pong, some were playing slippery games. Nine to ten-year-old children were running around and kicking the ball. And some were playing a game of chasing each other. The teenage boys were playing basketball with their friends on the basketball court.

Some of the young, middle-aged and older people were exercising, some were running lightly, and some were walking briskly in the park. Many were sitting on park benches enjoying their children's activities. Some were talking to each other. People with the same language and similar faces were exchanging identities with each other, while others were lost in thought.

In the park, he saw many Mexican-faced, Latin-Americans, some Chinese, a few Bengalis, and even blacks. He couldn't figure out the rest. And he saw some Nepalis too. But, only all the old people! *Maybe they have come to free themselves from the prison of the apartment to take their grandchildren to the park for a while!* He thought.

There will be no one at home. Even if they have a son and a daughter-in-law, they have gone to work at this time. Even if they have a daughter and a son-in-law, they have even gone to work. And how long will the husband stay in the room staring at the wife's face and the wife staring at the husband's face!

The weather would have to be good to come to the park with the baby! Not too cold, not too hot! In summer, you can relax in the park in the evening. Winter is a curse for New Yorkers! Moreover, for children and the elderly, it is not just a curse, it is a great punishment!

He meditated. *Is it for the son or daughter to take their parents on a tour of the United States from Nepal, or is it to take care of their child?* He became thoughtful.

Probably, everyone has their own interest and compulsion! Older people may also want to see the colorful world abroad. Older people will be happy to meet their children and grandchildren! On the other hand, if the parents were taken to the United States, the respect of relatives and

neighbors in Nepal would also increase! Here, again, the care of your child will be free! And if you arrange a ticket, it will be enough!

Again, even if there is a woman to look after the child, everyone has to pay at least one thousand or twelve hundred dollars a month. And then, there is the hassle of having to call from time to time to see if the working woman is looking after the baby properly!

Even when the child is kept in the day-care school, one person's time is wasted when the child is taken in the morning and brought in the evening. Even if you get a job somewhere in the afternoon, how much money can you make by working four or five hours?

Again, the son or daughter has not only brought their parents to America for their own selfishness, but love has also been mixed in it! In other words, it is as if both the warring factions have reached a mutual understanding by assuming that they will not be able to win the war completely and will have to bear a lot of losses even if they win! Let's say, silent agreement with each other without saying a word!

And if both husband and wife don't work, it's hard to live comfortably in New York! One person's income makes it difficult to support the whole family. Again, who doesn't have the greed to earn a little more money? Again, everyone has come to America by flying in the sky for so many hours to pick up the green dollar!

When we cultivate desire in our mind, we have to suffer from the weeds that grow along with desire! How can desire itself flourish without suffering at all?

The colonel came out of the dark tunnel of his own thoughts while thinking of others and took a deep breath, "Thankfully, I have never experienced anything like this in America!"

He was a colonel in the Royal Army at the time. It was not his desire, but the circumstances of the time that brought him to America. It was as if a hurricane had brought the roof of one village to another!

10

Lieutenant Rajendra Khadka took a two-week leave to prepare for the wedding. What should he prepare for the wedding? Brother, sisters-in-law, parents, sisters, relatives were all busy preparing for the wedding. All he had to do was show his presence in front of the bride!

The evening before going home, he gave a pre-party in the barracks, from the boss at the top to the bottom. He also verbally invited everyone to come to the wedding. He was sure that none of them would come to the wedding. Again, getting a leave in the army was not easy! So he gave a grand party with an open heart, thinking it was like a reception party after bringing the bride!

On the way home, he smiled a lot and was a little embarrassed too, imagining the day and night he would spend with his future wife.

There has been no dialogue. What to talk about the first night, how to sleep together in the same bed? How can I show my face in front of everyone the day after the wedding? He was ashamed to think so!

"It's not just me who has to face such a moment, it's a common problem that all brides have to face in life!" He made up his mind. At last, he looked confident.

When he got home, he saw that the wedding was in full swing.

Everyone was busy. Everyone was in a hurry. And everything needed for the wedding was arranged. The food was all ready. When he arrived, he saw some women whispering to each other and laughing. His face turned light red. He guessed that they must be talking about him.

He was also happy to see his family and relatives very happy. He was even more thrilled to think that everyone liked the bride. And his mind was convinced that his married life would be happy!

When he reached the bride's house with the procession, seeing the hospitality, welcome and respect shown by the bride's side, he also felt that the bride's family had accepted him happily!

The bride's uncle took him to the wedding hall with respect. The ancestral rites of marriage were conducted spontaneously by the Pandit. And at the same time, the bride was also present in the wedding pavilion.

He looked at his future wife's face. How could he see the bride's face, which was completely covered with a veil! Instead, the bride's makeup and the smell of new clothes added a kind of intoxication to his body.

The bride did not even look at him. He thought, *maybe she looked out of the corner of her eye!* Because his face was completely transparent, which could be easily seen by anyone.

He followed the Pandit's instructions completely, even though he was not satisfied with a few things. In any case, he followed the ritual completely. After all the wedding ceremonies were over, he was saddened to see the bride and her family members weeping.

The cry of the bride was justified when she had to leave the house where she was born and go to the house of the bridegroom! The cries of the bride's mother could not be lessened when her daughter, who had spent so many years together, was suddenly handed over to someone else! Why did blood relatives, relatives, friends, even neighbors fall behind, to shed their little tears while mixing rhythm in the lullaby of crying!

The groom's side hurried to take the bride, thinking that the crying would continue.

The bride sat in the back seat of the car with him. The bride's cousin sat next to her. And his sister-in-law sat in the front seat next to the driver.

He finally calmed down and breathed a sigh of relief. Anyway, the marriage went well.

Even being a bridegroom is a kind of torture! He felt. Going to the party is a comfortable pleasure for the guests, while being a bridegroom is just a hassle for the receptionist!

In any case, he also gathered the experience of being a bridegroom in life.

Along the way, the bride's physical touch made his body feel as different as his mind, which he had never felt before!

The early days of his marriage passed quickly. He felt as if two weeks had passed in two days. In any case, his mind was determined that his wife was cultured and practical. He assessed that she was more suitable to be the daughter-in-law of the house than his wife.

He spent two weeks sometimes visiting in-laws, sometimes visiting in-laws' houses, getting acquainted and having fun. His vacation was coming to an end as he could not fulfill his desire to share his feelings with his wife and to be alone with her. The new daughter-in-law was forced to work in the kitchen and outside! The order to please not only her husband but everyone in the house was received from her family in her dowry.

He was horrified to see such a chaotic atmosphere. Seeing his wife's busy schedule, he did not want to interfere with her unnecessarily. He thought that if he had to spend the rest of his life with his wife, why hurry now?

In such a long life, when you walk slowly, you can hear the melodious melody of life along with the footsteps!

On the day of his return to duty, he said goodbye to his family. And taking the opportunity to be alone, he hugged his wife and said, "I come to see you from time to time. Remember me! I love you!"

His wife was very shy, not a word came to her mouth to speak.

She could not say anything. If you spend a long time together, even words get a voice! In order for the heart to blend in with the heart, a dense dialogue between two hearts is needed!

His wife said, "I will stay at home. I don't go to my mother's house much. I'll wait for you to come."

He was very happy to think that his wife loved him very much.

His heart was not as happy in the barracks as before. The memory of his wife lingered in his eyes. The moments spent together danced in his memory. The memory of his wife haunted him even more. Anxiety about when to meet again lingered in his mind.

He spent less time at work, but more time in his wife's memory. He used to be too lazy to go home even on long vacations. He pretended not to go home. Instead, he would spend his days wandering around. Now time has changed direction. His heart and mind were no longer under his control! Given a chance, his mind would reach his wife's lap, like a bullet fired from a gun!

Anyway, he was in a hurry to go home on vacation. And the time spent with his wife was also extended. The family members were not surprised by the sudden change in him, they considered it natural. Instead, everyone turned the pages of their own past at once.

And so his days passed. Months passed. And years also passed. And new chicks were added to his family nest. After entering into the marital life, the religion of the household was automatically followed, even without any emphasis! Like it or not, the planets most orbit the sun!

Again, if there is no speed in life, what is the difference between a tree standing on the side of the road and a foot walking on the road!

At home, his wife was busy with household chores and taking care of the children. Along with the promotion in his job, his responsibility was also increasing. And he started to go home less and less.

I have fulfilled my family responsibilities. Again, even if I am not there, my wife has no problem raising a child in a joint family. There are many people in the house! He would ask himself ready-made questions and return ready-made answers. Say, prepare the question paper

yourself, and fill the answer sheet yourself!

Life went on at its own pace. Reckless! Happiness and sorrow, up and down, day and night came and went. Without any fuss!

He, too, was moving at his own pace. If there is a big storm on the way, start looking for shelter! Otherwise, why slow down? He was full of confidence that disasters and calamities would come without asking anyone and even if they did, he could face them.

He had a good trip today. Earnings also exceeded his expectations. *That's enough,* he thought. He stopped the car. He didn't even have to go around for parking. It was not difficult to get parking at 7 o'clock.

Without thinking left or right, his footsteps went straight to Jackson Heights. It was as if the restaurant had inserted magnetic chips into his feet while he was drunk!

He bought half a bottle of liquor from the liquor store and entered the Nepali kitchen as usual.

Someone you know can be found, even if not, Nepalis will be found! Time also passes by listening to them. You don't feel lonely at home, even if you drink alone! It seemed that his mind was explaining his complaint.

He went straight to the basement. Four or five of his acquaintances were drinking. Seeing him, the journalist shouted, "Oh, Colonel Saab! What's up after so many days? Come on, let's sit here!"

Everyone knew him, he didn't disobey. Pulling a side chair, he joined the crowd. And he shook hands with everyone. There was no question of missing Pasang. He was not only a regular customer of the kitchen but also a regular drunkard.

There was also a Chiring Sherpa. He only comes there two days a week, even with his wife's prior approval!

Dhakal was also there. He is also an Uber driver. Here he is single, if not to count the wife, son and daughter in Nepal!

While doing business in Nepal, Dhakal entered the United States with a loss and a debt. He has kept in mind the dream of getting a green card and enjoying his wife and children in the United States. Even late in the evening, he drinks a quarter of alcohol, eats food cooked in the Nepali kitchen, and goes into a room shared by four people. The slender body has no problem finding a place in the room!

In any case, Dhakal has his mind set on America. He has not let the dream die from his mind. The dream of a happy future is weaving in his mind!

The colonel poured the liquor into the glass and shook the glass and cheered everyone. He did not care about his old position, wealth and prestige. And again, if you talk about position and prestige, you will lose yourself! And again, here in the United States, who cares and who has the time to do research and talk about others?

In terms of seniors, getting a little bit of respect is a separate issue! Everyone knew the lesson taught by culture. Otherwise, why should one respect the other abroad? Everyone has work! They have earned by working according to their ability. Someone earns a lot, someone a little, that's a different matter. No one has to depend on anyone to drink alcohol. Everyone knows their quota, sometimes it has become normal to have a little more alcohol due to the pressure of friends.

Probably because of alcohol, the journalist started blabbering on, "Brother, did you read my article on online news? I have strongly refuted the work of the government. Call me anti-government, I don't care! Many people liked my article."

The journalist asked the colonel directly, not others. Maybe he thought others hadn't read it. Again, who has time to read articles in the United States, without counting dollars!

The colonel had read the article, but he did not find anything new. It was the same stale thing. The root of the problem was thoroughly explored, but the solution was not even a

hair's breadth. Let's say that even if the disease is detected, it is as if time is not wasted to find the method of treatment!

The colonel had something to say. And he said, "I like the article."

Why hurt others unnecessarily? Again, working abroad and worrying about your birth country's situation is not a heinous crime! The colonel thought a little emotionally. The journalist was happy, thinking that the colonel, like many others, liked his article.

Everyone was drunk. Pasang was more adept at laughing than speaking! He used to laugh in such a way that the germs of pain, problems and complaints were not born for him! Again, the tragedy of a life like his has hardly happened in the life of any customers who come to the Nepali kitchen!

Chiring doesn't drink much, but pours more alcohol into his friends' glasses. Whether it is out of fear of his wife or out of love, he is always in a hurry to get home. Also, if he doesn't get home before his wife comes home from work, his wife won't even bother to come to the Nepali kitchen! Slapping her husband on the cheek in front of everyone is not as difficult for his wife as fighting a guerrilla war!

What Chiring thought, he was in a hurry. And drinking the rest of the glass of alcohol at once, and surrendering himself in front of everyone, he said, "Now I go."

"You, bastard! You always hide your tail like a dog for fear of your wife. Coward! Instead, you would have been hiding in your wife's petticoat and drinking alcohol! Why did you have to come here out of fear? Your wife would be happy too!" Pasang made a very sarcastic remark.

Why did Chiring stay silent? He also immediately replied, "I don't have to live on the earnings of a wife like you. My wife is happy with me. I know how to make a woman happy. If

you obey your wife, everything will be fine! Why spoil a good relationship by arguing unnecessarily? After all, getting angry or arguing with your wife is like deliberately carrying a bag of stress on your shoulder!"

Chiring shared his own philosophy about married life.

"Such a man is called a bastard! Hiding in his wife's fur!" Pasang spoke even louder.

Feeling that the situation was still tense, the colonel concluded, "Trump seems to be ruining America's future! The future of immigrants like us will be even darker!"

Everyone's attention was drawn to the colonel's words. The atmosphere changed as the scene changed in the cinema. When the closed window of the room is suddenly opened, it is as if the air that has been suffocating for a long time has come out breathing a sigh of relief!

"It doesn't matter. Whether Trump's four-year term ends or not, it's unclear. There's been controversy from the beginning. Trump may even face impeachment!" The journalist shared his knowledge for free.

Everyone nodded in agreement. The colonel did not shake his head in agreement, nor did he move his tongue in disagreement.

The drinking atmosphere was still going on. Under the influence of alcohol, the volume of the noise was also increasing. Even though the light inside was very bright, the darkness was spreading its empire outside.

They do not go home soon. Half of the bottle of alcohol is dead but half is still alive! The colonel thought. And the colonel thought that it would be better to walk quietly under the pretext of urinating than to leave with everyone after completing the formalities. Then, the colonel came out without asking anyone.

After all, no one came here by informing anyone. Everyone came there to drink at their own pleasure. Say, there are people who share the table together until the drink! Even the colonel did not have the mobile numbers of any of them and did not know the names of many of them!

Like a face that is often met on the way to and from the office. Familiar by face, unfamiliar by name!

Captain Rajendra Khadka climbed another step and was promoted to Major Rajendra Khadka. New badge was added to his uniform. His chest widened. Happiness prevailed in the family. Relatives congratulated him! Neighbors praised him even if it was a show. Those who were jealous, burned inside. His wife was also promoted. Her value, respect and dignity increased among relatives, kinsmen and neighbors.

After becoming a major, he wanted to go to a more remote district than the city and become the commander of the whole platoon. He certainly did not choose to enjoy the beautiful and peaceful environment of the village, to enjoy the beauty of nature, to see the mountains as soon as he wakes up in the morning, and to climb the mountains in the evening. What he really needed was a life of dignity and honor!

He preferred to reprimand the juniors rather than bear the reprimand of the senior officers, even if he had to endure any obstacle! He put freedom at the top. Due to his position, it was not possible to get such facilities in the city, so he looked for a remote district. Even though the district was remote, everything was available inside the barracks!

He considered it appropriate to follow others under his own command rather than under the command of others. He wanted to enjoy complete freedom without stress, so he chose a hilly district. Posting near the house would have made him say 'no!' directly to his mind. He never gave in to his desires, dreams and freedom, no matter how much he lost. Again, he had never turned a profit and loss book in his life!

There was no question that he would not be warmly welcomed in the barracks. He was the commander of the battalion. Since everything had to be under his control, it was natural to mix respect and dignity in the reception. Again, it was like a tradition in the royal army.

He found the place as he thought. The mountains were clearly visible, the hill sides were also easy to climb. The river was like a swimming pool and the view of the greenery embraced from all sides was clearly visible to the naked eye. The barracks were also set up in an open space just above the city. From a security point of view, it was considered to be suitable for hilly districts.

His mind thought that even if he could not have any other fun, he could enjoy the beauty of nature.

He inspected the barracks from all sides. He also introduced all the soldiers. He also instructed everyone to observe the military discipline and conduct that must be followed.

He lay down on the bed and rested for a while. He was happy to see the dream that had been growing in his mind for years standing still like a shadow before his own eyes! He thanked his family deity from the bottom of his heart.

In the evening, he went for a walk inside the barracks. He walked around the barracks compound two or three times and went to rest on the bench. He beckoned to the soldier standing at a distance. The soldier approached and saluted. The dust on the ground there also flew far into the air. Major was very happy. This is what he sought and chose!

The major asked, "What are the arrangements for dinner?"

The soldier was very happy that the major had asked him for information and not with others.

In a single breath, he told the major, as if answering a general knowledge question he had memorized for the exam, "Knowing that you are coming here, everyone has organized a program in the evening. The soldiers entered the forest in the morning and killed the deer. They have also

arranged a good meal and dance, sir!"

In the evening, the colonel had just come out of the room wearing trousers, he saw a lot of activity in the meeting hall. And he went that way.

Everyone was waiting for him. Welcoming him, everyone requested him to reign on the sofa. Then the captain sat on one side of the other sofa and the lieutenant sat on the other side. Others took their seats according to their position.

He looked around. He saw seven people sitting in the middle of the hall. He also saw two girls among the five men. He recognized the boys as barracks soldiers here. But, girls! He was confused. *There are no vacancies for women here!* He thought to himself. Probably the soldiers had arranged for the dance from outside, his mind immediately guessed.

Suddenly the dancing started, he thought they were waiting for him. And with pride, his chest widened. Along with the deer meat, a bottle of whiskey also appeared on the table. The girls were also good at dancing. They were also beautiful. They didn't even look more than twenty- two or twenty- four years old. His heart was filled with joy, I have chosen the barracks very well!

The old men used to say, "Even when shooting an arrow in the dark, the target sometimes falls in the right place." His heart rejoiced.

Like a hen laying eggs to lay chickens, his mind also laid a sweet dream!

The colonel parked the car and turned on the Uber app on his mobile to see if there was any message to pick up the customer. It's been more than half an hour and no message has come on his mobile yet. People are attracted to trains instead of Uber! He talked to himself. It is not as expensive as a taxi and it can even reach the door of the house to pick up a passenger. However, income is declining rather than increasing!

Like others, he has been wondering why he is involved in driving from time to time. Sadness often bothers him; it is like the shadow of death bothers the patient of depression!

Disgusted by the mechanical diary of a sniffing clock, the thought of returning to Nepal without telling anyone would come to his mind from time to time. When he imagined the faces of his wife and children standing still like a wall in his path, his will power would be wasted!

And he was convinced that they are his world. And in his mind, he used to add energy again. In other words, it is like reviving a vehicle by servicing it in a workshop from time to time.

As if he was waiting patiently for the passenger, the urine was not waiting for him, the urine was asking for an exit! He looked around. He saw himself surrounded by large apartment buildings.

He felt as if the lock on the toilet door of a nearby public park was laughing at him! Seeing the toilet of the park closed in the evening, the hairs on his palate became very hot.

The colonel opened his mouth and said angrily, "Fuck! This country considers itself the most developed and powerful in the world! Why can't there be public toilets in many places? And even where it is somewhere, it is closed before evening! It's like being locked up before office hours, like a postal worker who doesn't earn money from anywhere under the table! Why can't New York, which never sleeps all night, keep the toilet open?"

He was not unaware that this was a common problem for all taxi and Uber drivers. Still, from time to time, his inner anger and sorrow would clash with each other. After the outburst of anger and grief, a spark of anger began to burn in his heart. And the same spark of anger moved from his heart to his mouth. And then the spark of anger would suddenly spill out of his mouth and explode!

The common experience that all professional drivers have to go through, where they can escape without experiencing it themselves, in New York, the busiest city in the world!

The colonel again entered the abyss of contemplation. Also, if you go to a restaurant and urinate, you have to buy tea and coffee first. There is a sign on the toilet door saying, 'Only for customers!' Even when parking a car, you have to put money in the machine. It costs at least two or three dollars to urinate once. The question of how many times a day to urinate, how many times to pay the money blocks your way and asks you for an answer! Instead, you should drink less water and urinate less throughout the day, this is the economical way for everyone to adopt!

The colonel's mind was ablaze, remembering what the SP had said when he had already met him in the Nepali kitchen. The SP was right. However, the colonel did not agree with the SP, thinking that it would offend his ego. His mind had tacitly agreed. That was what he was experiencing. Where did he need the advice and suggestions of others?

The colonel wondered why he got involved in driving. Again, in his old age, he would have put out the fire that was burning in his mind to find another job. No matter how much you take out the grievances that have accumulated in your heart, in the end, you would have to enter the real world! Practical compulsion would have opened its mouth like a dragon! In fact, it would be better for anyone to go his own way than to tease the dragon!

In other words, the situation is like a criminal surrendering to the police station thinking that it is better to stay in jail than to commit suicide when there is no way to escape!

He got out of the car, inserted the ATM card in the machine and dropped the parking ticket. The ticket was placed in front of the windshield inside the car so that the traffic could easily see it. And he locked the car remotely. 'Plick!' And he went to a nearby hospital. He entered the toilet of the hospital which was open twenty-four hours a day. No one's restraint, no one's concern! He went out after doing biological work in the toilet.

He came to the street and lit a cigarette. Just as a meditating yogi smokes marijuana in his spare time, he also started smoking. He felt relieved after smoking.

He was about to go to the parking lot when someone said, "Colonel Saab!"

He heard the call, near the gate of the hospital. He felt as if he had heard the voice before, as if he was a familiar person.

When he looked back, he saw the same well-known contractor, Bikram Thapa! He was the contractor of the district where he was posted when he was an army major! Even after he was transferred from the district, his friendship with Thapa remained till later.

Thapa, a clever local contractor of the district, also of 'A' class! He used to have good relations with the big bosses and leaders of the district. When a new officer was transferred to the district police, army or administration, he was the first one to greet. He was hospitable. Who doesn't like welcome and hospitality! Everyone fell in love with him.

He did not have to run in front of everyone's eyes like in a marathon to win a contract in and around the district. The setting would have won him over. He did not need the blessings of any accomplished Mahatma to adjust the interior setting. He himself was perfect in such work!

The local goons were after him. Otherwise, how could they arrange money and motorcycles to have fun, drink and hang out with girlfriends! And as the election approached, local leaders saw no other way out than to turn to him for help.

He did not serve, selflessly; he had his own selfishness! He also needed a strong ladder to climb.

The contractor was a little surprised and very happy to see the colonel suddenly in a foreign country. The colonel's mood was similar.

"It's amazing! In such a big world, there is a sudden encounter! Scientists say the earth is round! It really is!" Contractors who undertake big projects have to be adept at talking.

"I never thought I'd meet you like that. Are you here in New York?" The colonel also asked in surprise.

"It's in Jackson Heights, 82nd Street," the contractor said.

"I also live on 79th Street near Elmhurst Hospital. I've never met you, even though it's close to where I live," the colonel asked in surprise.

"The restaurant works twelve hours a day, that too six days a week! One day off, I used to sleep a lot that day. I have to do laundry again. I don't have time to go out. And what do you do?" The contractor expressed his grief along with his busy schedule.

"I run Uber. We couldn't meet each other because of the nature of our work!" The colonel whispered, as if he had found some serious philosophy in the definition of life.

"You have a lot of free time. You can go to work whenever you want, otherwise you can rest at home. You don't have to follow the clock like us!"

The colonel could not easily guess whether the contractor had fired a sarcastic arrow or

something in his mind. He didn't even care. In other words, he didn't want to hurt his head by hitting it on the wall.

Instead, he politely asked the contractor, "Have you come to the hospital for a checkup?"

"I had an appointment with the doctor today. The checkup is over. Now I have free time. And are you busy? Otherwise, we have met after so many years! Do you want to sit in a restaurant and share our sorrows and joys? What do you think? Colonel Saab!" The contractor also made a proposal by mixing the request.

The colonel didn't deny it either, a man with such an old acquaintance! He also remembered the fun parties he had with him. And the hospitality he provided also came to his mind.

Rejecting his request for two or four hundred dollars is like trying to sell a cow that always used to give four liters of milk and today, gave only two liters!

He put the contractor in the car and searched for parking around his house. Again, he thought that the time limit would be forgotten in the drinking environment. Which he had experienced from time to time. He just needed free parking. There would be an ultimatum of two hours if placed in pay-parking, otherwise the traffic would have given the ticket.

Again, you don't even know that a couple of hours have passed while drinking alcohol, no matter what the place and the environment! That's why, even though it took time, he still needed safe parking.

If one has the patience and effort, sooner or later he will find what he is looking for, just as he finally found the parking lot, a walking distance of twenty-five minutes from home. He smiled thinking that there would be a morning walk tomorrow even if he didn't want to.

Most people, no matter how many failures they get in their endeavors, celebrate the small success in the end as a big victory! Wrapping up a lot of failures with a small handkerchief of success, people are overwhelmed!

The colonel also considered his victory in the end. And without thinking anything left or right, the colonel took the contractor and headed for the Nepali kitchen.

15

The colonel followed the same old routine. He entered the liquor store, bought alcohol and went to the Nepali kitchen.

Before going to the basement, the colonel ordered food at the counter above, "A plate of buffalo meat, a plate of mutton, a plate of roasted chicken, a plate of roasted soybeans, as well as mashed potatoes!"

He knew that when he went to the basement to order, the food would arrive a little late, and he knew another advantage. When ordering in front of the owner, as a regular customer, even if there was no difference in quality, there was a slight difference in quantity!

The contractor was surprised to find out that most of the food available at local restaurants in Nepal were available here! Despite being so close, he regretted not getting any information about this Nepali kitchen. The contractor regretted that he had become like a frog in a well!

Now the contractor regretted working in a restaurant! Always the same Indian food! When I was tired of eating tandoori roti, naan, chicken tandoori, chicken tikka masala, butter mutton curry, chicken biryani, spinach cheese, samosa, chaat, rose berries, mango lassi, masala tea, etc., it was a pleasure to taste Nepali food!

Again, he became very angry with himself, for running after

money with both eyes closed!

However, the contractor did not say anything in front of the colonel. The colonel could smile at his ignorance. He could imagine how stupid he was! The colonel could have thought that not only in Nepal but also in the United States, the ghost of money had not left him. The contractor thought to himself that it is hundred times better to hide your weakness than to show it!

Again, weakness is not like smoke that cannot be hidden! With this in mind, he followed the colonel to the basement.

The contractor was shocked again, seeing that only all Nepalis had gathered! It was as if they had gathered for a party!

Probably because it was evening, he saw that there were bottles of drinks on most of the tables. He found that beer cans occupied more space on the tables than coke cans. Only a few women were eating dumplings, noodles, Nepali bread and vegetables. Some were enjoying Nepali local food. Some were busy eating and some were busy talking. Most were busy drinking!

The colonel saw the corner table empty. He thought it appropriate to stay there, it would be easier to talk and less disturbing. The colonel asked the boy for some ice and two glasses. As he ordered at the counter above, snacks also started coming. The colonel poured large pegs of whiskey into both glasses and two pieces of ice into both glasses.

"Well, cheers! After a long time!" The colonel first picked up the glass and the contractor slammed his glass against the colonel's glass, "Cheers!"

"Didn't you come to America in 2003 or 2004?" The colonel inquired.

"Ah, in 2004," the contractor replied embarrassingly. Suppose he didn't want to get into this topic.

"You had such a good life in Nepal. You earned a lot. You got along well with big people. You had a luxurious life. You had a lifestyle like the Aristocrats. And why did you come to America all of a sudden?" Intoxicated or out of curiosity, the colonel asked in one breath.

The contractor was stunned. He thought for a moment and said,

"What can I say? The door of my heart is still closed. The key to opening the door has not been found yet. Let's get drunk first and then open the door of the heart completely, Colonel Saab!"

He became a philosopher in an instant and swallowed a long peg in one breath.

"Let's add a couple of pegs first. There's still a lot to talk about!" The contractor was adept at giving eloquent answers.

The habit from childhood is not so easy to get rid of, no matter where you are in the world! Improving the habit of a leader who always gives false assurances seems to be more difficult than freeing a drug addict from drug addiction!

Both of them drank alcohol one by one. And their old days were getting fresh. Those funny moments came to mind. In winter, the rays of the sun deceive the eyes of the fog and look at the earth from time to time!

The contractor was so drunk that he suddenly became angry, "Bastard! The Maoists took me from the palace to the street at once. It took me less than seven months to lose all the economic progress and social prestige I had achieved in seven years!"

The contractor was opening. The story of the colonel was the same, even though the experience was different. The time and circumstances were the same. Otherwise, why would he leave the glory and honor he got in his homeland and come to America like an unseasonable storm!

The colonel said nothing about himself, just focused on the contractor. Suppose the colonel has to write a book after finding out everything about the contractor's emigration to the United States!

"Colonel Saab! You know very well about me, don't you? It's the same district where you were posted when you were a major! Our district was also one of the districts most affected by the Maoist conflict, wasn't it?" The contractor paused.

The contractor drank half a glass of whiskey in one gulp. And all of a sudden, he raised his voice and said, "That bastard! He used to have fun with my money. I had to bear the cost of his alcohol and the girls. The bastard joined the Maoist party and threatened me and asked for donations. Not a penny less than two million rupees! He also said that he had reduced it by recommending from above!"

Instead of pouring water to soothe the arousal of the mind, he thought it appropriate to pour alcohol, so he swallowed the rest of the glass of whiskey in one breath and thought for a while.

In any case, whether it was due to the magic of alcohol or something else, the volume of his voice has decreased a lot now. And the contractor now said calmly, "I also said angrily, I don't want to donate to your party as much as possible. But, if you bring the party's letter and receipt, I can donate up to two lakhs rupees at most."

The contractor was silent for a moment, reached for the bottle and put a peg in his glass. And calming down again, he said, "That bastard threatened me back and said, 'Understand! whatever the consequences may be!' and he went berserk."

The contractor was silent for a long time. The colonel did not even ask the contractor why he was silent. The colonel also reached for the glass, wondering what to do at break time. He shook the glass of whiskey that had been sleeping for some time. And in one breath, he swallowed the whiskey.

He didn't have to say anything, the contractor started on his own. Let's say, after the engine of the car heats up a lot, we put it in a cool place for a while to cool down and then we start and drive again!

"After that, the Maoists started obstructing my work. They went to the project site and

threatened the workers, vandalized the goods, demolished the structure and destroyed it. However, they set fire to the parked excavator. I had bought the property by leasing my house and land and taking a loan from a bank. Then, my life went downhill as if I couldn't climb uphill like a car with brake failure, so I went straight downhill!" The contractor looked very sad.

And the contractor slowly picked up the bottle from the table and said sadly, "My life has been empty like this bottle of whiskey. No? it was full before, now it's empty!"

The contractor became very emotional and serious. The colonel did not speak, but became thoughtful.

After a while, the contractor took a deep breath and said, "It was okay to lose my property, real estate, business. I earned it myself, I lost it myself! While working, I also pledged my in-laws' house in the bank! In-laws' house had to be brought back from the bank anyway! And the loan had to be repaid!"

The contractor paused and breathed a sigh of relief. "Fortunately, once I came to the United States for a construction seminar, I arranged a visa for my wife. There was still time for multiple visas. We, the husband and wife, came to the United States secretly without the knowledge of anyone except the in-laws, leaving the children in the care of the in-laws."

The contractor took a deep breath. He swallowed the rest of the glass of whiskey and ended the story by saying, "I don't have to tell you the rest of the story. You also experienced it yourself already!"

The contractor did not look as sad or worried as before. He has completely surrendered himself. He has given his life to the tide of time. Wherever the tide of time blows, so does it. Reckless!

In the pleasant atmosphere of the mountains, Major's routine went on as if the autumn sun was moving comfortably, no clouds, no fog!

He was so overwhelmed that even the memory of his family stuck in the back of his mind. In the past, he did not care so much about home, wife and children, but it does not mean that he ignored them. He never neglected his family responsibilities. And not that he didn't have an attachment to his family. He loved to carry family responsibilities as well as to rejoice with the desires that were rising like waves in his mind!

"Family responsibilities are in their place, which is not easy to get rid of, but why make the moment tasteless by just thinking about it!" This was Major's strongest philosophy.

He was a staunch follower of this path. Moreover, the atmosphere here, the fun, the freedom, the value, the respect had completely swallowed him. Trapped in all these things, he became absorbed in this environment like an ascetic.

"Sir! Someone has called you," the colonel's sleep was suddenly disturbed by the soldier's husky voice.

"Major Saab! Why are you sitting in the barracks on Saturday too? Come to my quarters, let's enjoy playing cards," he recognized the CDO (Chief District Officer)'s voice.

He also liked the offer. *Why stay alone in the barracks on holiday!* He thought. Again, even mingling with his juniors did not seem reasonable in terms of his rank. "Well, I'll be there soon," he said on the phone.

By the time he arrived, everyone had gathered. DSP (District Superintendent of Police), DFO (District Forest Officer), Land Revenue Officer, two or three others he did not know. Maybe they're CDO assistants, he guessed. When he arrived, the number needed to play cards was also met. Didn't they call me because they lacked a man to play cards with? His mind doubted.

When he saw a bottle of black label whiskey, cashew nuts, pistachios, and mutton on the table, his mind calmed down, as if pouring cold water on a burning firewood!

He used to enjoy playing cards while drinking, eating, joking and laughing. However, he considered it useless to play cards just to make money. So he didn't really enjoy gambling. He tried to stay away from such gatherings as much as possible. He would join such an environment only to accept the request of others.

Alcohol got into everyone's veins. The evening was about to disappear into the dark alley, perhaps the evening was in a hurry to have intercourse with the night! Everyone went to their nests as if to say, "Even if the day is for themselves, the night is for the arms of the sleeping goddess!"

He also left with everyone and went to the barracks. Not wanting to enter the room directly, he entered the canteen. He saw everyone eating and going to their rooms. And the two soldiers were still eating. Seeing him, the boy in charge of the canteen came running.

"Shall I bring you food, Sir?" The boy asked politely.

"It's not time to eat right now. Instead, take a quarter of whiskey," the major ordered in a military manner. The alcohol he had drunk before had disappeared from his body.

The boy immediately brought a quarter of whiskey. The Major poured a large peg of whiskey into a glass. And he poured a little water and took a slow sip. He was in no hurry except to go to bed and sleep.

He lit a cigarette and meditated for a while. He also forgot his cigarette and the alcohol on the table. Perhaps he was engrossed in something more pleasurable than alcohol and cigarette smoke!

Unexpectedly, the family rose in his memory. Suppose a son who has been missing for years suddenly appeared in the yard!

It's been a long time since I've been home, he thought. *It has been almost two years since I was posted here. I went home only three or four times in between,* he recalled. *Anyway, I have called from time to time. I have also sent the money from time to time by giving it to those who go home on holiday. I have been asking about everything at home. If something bad happened, someone from home would inform me anyway and call me to come home if needed!* He argued with himself to explain his mind. This is the job of the army, where it is not enough to look after the responsibilities of the family, the responsibility of the country must also be fulfilled!

He swallowed a glass of whiskey, as if his flight was about to take off! The cigarette did not wait for him like alcohol, the cigarette was already asleep.

He poured a peg of whiskey into the glass, adding a little water. He didn't rush to drink now, but put the sleeping cigarette in the ashtray. He took another cigarette from the packet and lit it. And he smoked a cigarette to make a small spark of fire. He blew a long smoke. He saw the smoke running down the ceiling. And the smoke suddenly disappeared without a trace.

"All human beings must one day disappear from the world like this smoke!" He was surprised by such a reclusive thought. Maybe he got too drunk!

He gestured to the same boy to divert his attention. The boy came running.

"Prepare the food by heating it," the major ordered.

The major swallowed a glass of whiskey. And the rest of the bottle was poured into a glass. He had to wait ten or fifteen minutes for the food to arrive.

One morning the major woke up terrified. His whole body was drenched in sweat. He slowly opened his eyes. Hey, it's a dream! He breathed a sigh of relief.

He had not forgotten the dream he had seen in the morning. He was hunting alone in the dense forest with a gun. He saw a deer. He was about to shoot the deer so that it would not move. Amazing! About ten or fifteen deer from all around had surrounded him. All the deer were staring at him. Now he was confused as to which deer to shoot first.

Apparently, the deer turned into human beings, just as Ravana assumed the form he wanted in the Ramayana! Not all the boys looked over twenty-two years old. Everyone had a gun in their hand and the butt of the gun was pointed at him. He became paralyzed! He was scared. And seizing the opportunity, he tried to escape. But his legs did not support him! The legs became lame. He ran to save his life with those paralyzed legs.

He also realized in a dream that man uses all his remaining power to save his life. Again, the dreamer thinks that the dream is real until he wakes up!

He kept running with all his strength in his body, but the boys were about to find him. He did not see any solution. Nearby he saw a cliff. He thought that it would be better to jump off a cliff and die at once than to die hundreds of times after being tortured by boys. And he jumped off the cliff.

He woke up suddenly before he saw himself on the brink of death. He was relieved that it was a dream, but he did not take the dream lightly.

He was worried that he would hear bad news. He believed in the signs of dreams. Not once, but many times the dream would have told him in advance what would happen next. He thought that at least ninety percent of his dreams would come true.

The hang of the dream he saw in the morning haunted him. His sleep was now completely broken. Sleep is far away now; it will not return soon. Sleep may come to stay with me only at night! He smiled at his strange thoughts.

Is the light still asleep or what? Why did it take so long to fall to the ground? He also lay on the bed feeling lazy. He changed the channel on the radio and tried to listen to the news on FM. Most of the FMs were broadcasting religious songs, hymns and sermons. His finger did not stop at any channel. But, in one channel, his finger suddenly rested.

"Today's breaking news! We have just received information that the Maoists attacked three or four police outposts at the same time last night and looted weapons. We do not have any information about the exact number of casualties. Details will be available in another bulletin." The woman's loud voice was heard. And again, the same religious discourse began. He turned off the radio.

Gradually, the Maoists were stepping up their attacks on police outposts in remote areas across the country.

He did not understand what the Maoists were trying to do. By attacking the police station, looting a small number of weapons, gathering an army of two or four thousand young men and women, they marched to capture the state! He laughed to himself. That is how the state is captured! If the army is to be deployed, it will not take even a week to eliminate the Maoists!

By attacking small police posts, the Maoists may have thought that they have done a great job! With only eight or ten policemen on duty, with unused rusty weapons, all asleep at night under the influence of alcohol, and with the mindset that surrendering without retaliation would save

life, it became easier for them to capture the outpost! The major acted as if he was angry with himself, not with others.

He became a little more aware. He wondered why he was beating his own chest in the anger of others. Now he turned to the police. Bastards! You always harass and frighten the poor villagers! You ever look down on the daughters and daughters-in-law of the villagers, and you often do disgusting things when you get the chance! Damn! It is because of your heinous act that many villagers have joined the Maoists to vent their anger and revenge!

What do they understand about Marxism and Maoism, who have passed only five or seven classes? The colonel expressed doubts. If it is difficult for a person with an MA in Political Science to understand Marx's books well, how can they understand? Again, he was angry with himself.

After a while, he returned to his old position. Now it was the turn of the Maoists. Fucking Maoists! You have shown a big dream that is difficult to see even in a dream to the children of poor people during the day! You have dreamed of capturing the country by gathering innocent children of poor people!

What will happen to them if the army is only ordered to leave the barracks? They may have thought that by attacking a few police stations, they may one day be able to win the state! He felt sorry for the Maoists.

He went into the bathroom, wondering why he was thinking so much about such an unnecessary thing. And freshened up, he walked out of the room.

The sun was slowly rising, trampling the top of the mountain with its golden feet!

The major sat down on the bench and asked for tea. And then he started talking to himself. Drinking tea in the warm morning sun is another fun! The plane has not brought the magazine yet!

Otherwise, drinking tea and reading magazines is even more fun! A good combination!

After drinking tea, he was walking inside the compound. He saw a postman coming from the other side. The postman was about to go to the office room to deliver the letters, so he gestured to him to come to his place.

He glanced at the letters brought by the postman. All the letters were related to the work of the barracks, not personal letters. At last, he saw an envelope with an urgent stamp, which was named after him!

He took the envelope in his name, asking the postman to hand over the rest of the letters to the office. With a little curiosity and a lot of apprehension, he tore the envelope and took out the letter and read it.

He felt dizzy. He felt as if the ground had been washed away and he was being carried to the womb of the earth! It was as if a storm had blown off the roof of a house and taken him to some remote place!

Why shouldn't he feel that way? Someone suddenly poured a bucket of acid on all his happiness, dreams, desires, aspirations, and the meaning of life!

In his hand which was his transfer letter! In which it was written, to appear at the headquarters within fifteen days anyway!

18

"The tea is on the table. It's getting cold now. Get up!" His wife's loud voice woke him up. The wall clock had already crossed the ten-minute journey at eight o'clock.

He always got up before seven o'clock. He always made tea for his wife. He always followed the same routine. Today it was amazing, the opposite happened! He was surprised. His wife prepared tea for him.

I went to bed early yesterday, he wondered why I woke up late. I don't even feel like I went out yesterday, I feel like drinking a little at home. If I drank a lot yesterday, I should have listened to my wife's loud speech in the morning, but she didn't! Various things started conversing with his mind.

Last night, it seemed to be deleted from my mind, he thought. The thing that has been deleted in our mind cannot be taken out of the junk box like a computer and restored again! I would still be asleep if my wife didn't wake me up, he murmured to himself. It is not that he did not experience such a blank state when he drank too much sometimes. Anyway, nothing bad happened, he breathed a sigh of relief.

He sat on the bed and started drinking tea. And he opened the laptop. He started searching online newspapers to see if there was any new news in Nepal.

It was the same stale news that kept repeating as usual. Minister's speech! Inauguration of new project and laying of foundation stone! Road accidents! Minor girl raped! Husband killed wife! Wife killed husband for boyfriend! Abduction! Ransom! Corruption! Released on bail! Government employee arrested for taking bribe! Demonstration in front of Parliament House! Fasting to death! Dance bar raid! Threat to start movement! Long line to go for foreign employment! Human trafficking! Women held hostage abroad by brokers! Illegal gold seized at airport! The stock market fell again!

He only looked at the news like this, but he did not enter the details of the news.

This is the reality of our country! When will the day come to run a system like here! He sighed. And turning off his laptop and sipping tea, he lost himself in the world of thought.

"You know? Today our daughter is going to visit Vegas with friends. She has two weeks off work." He felt like his wife had said before.

He would not take such a thing seriously. When you are young, you have to travel to new places, try different types of food, and have fun with your friends. And as you get older, your desires shrink automatically! He thought so. At a young age in life, you have to experience everything, and you become mature! He had even allowed his children to recite this mantra of his life.

His wife was ready to go to work. The daughter was busy packing the bag. The son may still be sleeping, he guessed. He did not know when his son came home yesterday. He himself was drunk, and he slept without eating.

Hesitantly, he said to his wife, who was busy preparing, "Our children have grown up now. They can earn their own living and make their own decisions about life. From time to time we come here to visit our children. Let's go to Nepal! There is also a house to live in. My pension will also come. It has been almost two years since it was taken. Let's spend our retired life in Nepal!"

He has memorized this dialogue more than a hundred times, as if Hanuman Chalisa has been memorized by Hanuman's devotees!

And in response, he also remembered the dialogue that his wife always used to tell him.

"Even if I die, I will not go to Nepal. If you want to go, go! I have nothing to say. Before you go, you have to divorce me. Then we will have no relationship. Understood?"

He has not been able to find out for sure whether his wife has reprimanded him or threatened him. Suppose, reprimands and threats are mixed in such a way that even God's magical power to separate them from each other is not enough!

In response from his wife, he knew that he would always be silent in the end. But still, like throwing a stone in a calm pool and watching the water wave, sometimes he would try to look inside his wife's mind, to see if the color of change could be seen somewhere!

Even though he didn't find anything in his wife's mind, he found a dark cloud of despair in his mind, and he was full of thoughts.

After all, he could not have left his wife alone, nor could he have given up all the comforts of life and risked living alone in Nepal!

What can I do alone in Nepal! Nor is it possible to bring another wife at this age! There are all the families here, but in Nepal there is neither my mother nor my father! Brothers have their own world! Thinking about such things, he used to apply a balm of consolation to reduce the fever of the mind.

He was forced to stay in the United States against his will. However, he also had to ride the rickshaw of life by speeding on the smooth ground, driving slowly on the downhill, and pushing hard on the uphill!

Life has to be moving, not stable! It should flow like a river. Sitting on the riverbank like a rock and watching the water wave and imagining 'where it will rest' does not fit the definition of life at all!

So quietly talking to himself, he walked on the path of life at his own pace. And in the hiding of day and night, he remained a silent spectator!

Speaking of his return to Nepal, he was well aware that his wife's mood would deteriorate. Nevertheless, he was addicted to raising such issues in front of his wife from time to time. Like a bumper lottery! Always hope, meet disappointment!

"When I come home, I tell you not to get drunk. I want to talk when you are fresh. Talking to a drunken man at night, even in small things, fights start. As soon as I get up in the morning, I hurry to go to work. One day off a week, I spend all day cleaning, cooking, and laundry! And when to talk to you?"

His wife started grumbling. He understood that it was a reaction to his return to Nepal.

"After drinking with friends in the Nepali kitchen, you always insist that you return to Nepal! Who gives you such advice there? Rascal!" The wife closed the door and came out muttering angrily.

As the sound of his wife's shoes slowly faded, he got out of bed. To regain his composure, he opened a bottle of whiskey from the cupboard, poured a peg of whiskey into a glass, and poured a little water. And in one sip, he emptied the whole glass.

I don't go to work today, I will do double duty tomorrow! He spoke softly to his mind. Suppose, his mind is very angry with him for drinking alcohol instead of going to work and he has to convince the angry mind anyway!

He still did not understand why women do not want to hear about returning to Nepal after

coming to the United States! This was not only his context, but also the curiosity and

grievances of most of the men at his gatherings.

Husbands want to return to Nepal, women do not accept even if they die. Amazing!

19

The next day after receiving the transfer letter, he packed his bags and headed for the airport. Giving his junior the necessary responsibilities and instructions, he quietly left without telling anyone. He did not consider it necessary to give a farewell party to anyone. He left without meeting the CDO or DSP.

Leaving the place where he had spent almost two years, he disappeared like a whirlpool. Suppose a guest arrives without informing you, as if he leaves without informing you!

Leaving the mountains, the hills, the greenery, the streams, the local liquor, the village girls, the respect inside and outside the barracks, the hospitality, and the freedom, he left quietly.

In his heart he carried the burden of emptiness, even in the barracks he sowed emptiness. Everyone missed him for a long time!

When he got home, he spent most of his time sleeping. There was plenty of time to show up at the center. Why hurry! Which district should I be sent to later or should I just spend time at the headquarters? He didn't think much about it because it was a headache.

He spent a week with his family. He was interested in his children's education. He glanced at the children's certificate for the first time. The children were moderate in their studies. The children did not work hard or the result was not good because I was not interested in their studies! He abused himself rather than blaming others. Now I have to be fully responsible for the family, the old way no longer works! He made up his mind.

In the evening, he was lying on the bed when his uncle appeared in the yard.

"Ah, Rajendra! I don't know if you have come home. You haven't even shown your face to anyone! Do you just hang out with your wife day and night or what? You don't have to meet us. We have to go looking for you?" Uncle suddenly shouted.

He jumped out of bed and got out.

"No, uncle! I have done a lot of work in the district and now I am resting at home. I stay at home to pay attention to my children's education." He explained his compulsion to his uncle as if he had given an explanation to a boss of a higher rank. And he asked his uncle, "Uncle, should I ask my wife to make tea?"

"Does anyone have tea in the evening too? We've just met after a long time. I thought you'd offer me a drink, but you're talking about having tea! What's the matter with you?" He understood his uncle's intention to come here. Aunty doesn't even let uncle touch alcohol at home. Uncle came here wanting to drink! He guessed.

"No, Uncle! I heard that you had given up the drink, otherwise I would have sent someone to call you yesterday!" He expressed his ignorance.

Going inside, he took a bottle out of the drawer and said to his son, "Bring two glasses first. And tell Mummy to heat the meat and fry the soybeans." Obeying his direct orders, the son went to the kitchen.

The wife greeted the uncle and placed the fried meat, soybeans and cucumber on the table. Then, uncle and nephew's cheers for alcohol started. Uncle and nephew were not much different in age. In total, five or seven winter uncles' bodies might have suffered more! He didn't have to worry about where to start the conversation.

Uncle started the conversation, probably drunk, "I heard you were transferred. Why did they suddenly drag you to the center before your period ended? You are a bit rude. I think they are sending you to Maoist-influenced areas. Now the Maoist attacks are intensifying in the villages. All the police posts have been demolished! They have a monopoly in the village. I don't understand what they are trying to do! Of course, they have not touched the army yet. What can be said is that they moved forward at the same pace! Tell me, Rajendra! What do you think?"

Uncle talked for a long time. Suppose, he was an army officer himself and was very worried that his life would be eclipsed!

He said according to his thinking and temperament, "Nothing is going to happen. It is foolish of them to think that they will occupy the state by vacating a few police posts. If they touch us, they are finished! Like cold drying in the sun, like a pond drying in summer! This revolution is nothing but a game to deceive and provoke the poor and helpless people. It is a way for the leaders to make a good living by forcibly collecting donations from the people. Understand? uncle!"

His body became very hot due to his drunkenness and intense anger towards the Maoists, but after expressing his bitterness, his mind became very cold. As my uncle said, I was called to the head-quarters to be deployed in a remote Maoist-affected district, didn't I? Suspicion fluttered in his mind.

20

As he suspected, he was transferred to a Maoist-affected area. Well, the Maoists had not yet launched a major military offensive in the area.

The General handed him the transfer letter and told him, "Rajendra! You are brave and fearless! You have also received commando training. Now we need skilled and trained soldiers like you. Looking at the actions of these traitorous terrorists, it seems that they have great ambitions. Therefore, the recent high-level meeting has passed that the armies should also remain alert. Specifically, I hired you for this job. You stay in the remote area for some time. It is now my responsibility to make you a colonel. Who can dare to disobey my recommendation? You know."

Though he had some doubts and dissatisfaction in his mind, the greed for promotion immediately reigned in his mind. His mind was cleansed and healed, as if the dirty clothes he had been wearing for months had been wiped off with soap and water in an instant!

There was nothing he could do. Again, disobeying his boss was tantamount to violating military discipline!

Instead, to appease the general, he said, "I have always followed your advice. You considered me worthy of such a job. That is a great reward for me!"

"Well, get ready to go soon. If you need anything, call me directly. You don't have to think left or right, you know? You drink a little too much, reduce it." The general gave a commanding instruction by hitting him on the back with a balloon filled with a little color of love!

Giving some time to his family, he decided to go to a remote district. His mind had already predicted that he would not have a happy life like before.

Life is not always a straight path! Where all the roads are the same! Sometimes life has to take a crooked path! Otherwise, life becomes monotonous, dull, boring! Let's just say that living is not the only essence of life!

After saying goodbye to his family and friends, he left for a new place, to continue his duties in a new environment. Again, after receiving the salary of the state, it was the responsibility of the citizen to do the work assigned by the state.

He was also reminded by his family and relatives when he left, "Be careful, be alert! Don't be too rude, be restrained. Time, situation is not right now!" He also memorized the exhortation in his heart.

The barracks were in a remote place, just the opposite of what he had imagined. Not like the city, not the whole village environment! From the day he arrived, he began to feel sad. The atmosphere was completely deserted. Before evening, all the shops were closed. People's activity was almost zero. Probably due to the influence of the Maoists here, he also felt their dominance, terror, intimidation and interference. He had also heard that they had announced a people's government in the village.

He came to know that there was a state and a government only in the district headquarters.

His barracks also served as a night shelter for CDO and district officials. There was only fear and terror in everyone. He did not find any enthusiasm in the army. Everyone seemed to be languishing like a chicken eating salty food made to feed the cattle. The enthusiasm and vigor that should have been in a soldier seemed to be lost somewhere!

Time is not running out properly, there is definitely something wrong. The coming days will be worse than expected! His conscience prophesied.

"Major Saab! Not to drink? I can't sleep without drinking it. I don't know if I will survive

tomorrow or not! The police and the CDO are the main targets of the Maoists. They don't dare much during the day, but what about at night? How can I sleep confidently in a quarter with a couple of clumsy cops! Anyway, the armies are here and so the night passes peacefully. Otherwise, where will I hide and save my life at night? " If the CDO of the district had his own kind of fear and terror, what about the general public? He imagined.

The CDO had brought a bottle of liquor. What did he have to do in this desolate place? He also needed a man who talked while drinking alcohol. As the dragon's food is provided by the gods, he also found a friend who sat and drank together in this barren place.

He thought that it would not be so difficult to spend the night. And his mind felt a little relief.

He asked the soldier standing nearby to bring some snacks, cold water and two glasses of whiskey.

The colonel looked at the time on his mobile. It was seven o'clock. After earning three hundred dollars, he thought it was enough for today. And he planned to park the car and walk to Jackson Heights. What to drink alone at home! Be with someone while drinking! Even if there is no one, there is an atmosphere to spend time listening to others! Thinking like this, he searched for a parking lot and found it easily.

And he went straight to the same Nepali kitchen, like a horse with a bandage tied on both sides of his eyes!

He bought half a bottle of whiskey from the liquor store and entered the Nepali kitchen. He saw a journalist, Pasang, Lama, Nawaraj, Dhakal and two or three others drinking while putting two tables in one place.

"Come on, Colonel Saab! Let's sit here," the journalist pulled up a side chair.

He didn't even have to open the bottle he had brought. Pasang asked for a glass, opened the bottle of whiskey on the table, and poured out a nice peg. And he added a little water and held the glass in the colonel's hand. The colonel slammed the glass and cheered everyone.

Everyone was a little drunk. The restaurant was also full. All in their own tune, all in their own rhythm!

The colonel knew about the journalist's family life. After drinking alcohol together several times, the journalist told him his story. The journalist's ten-year relationship with his wife had turned into a divorce. Because of the divorce, he had no one else but his best friend. That friend shared an apartment with him. In the absence of sustainable work and accommodation, he provided free shelter and food to the friend.

One day when he returned home from work in the afternoon feeling unwell, he found his wife and his best friend in his bed, almost completely naked. Without saying a word, he returned the same way. It's like a situation where you think of your own room and sneak into other people's rooms and come out saying 'I'm sorry!'

He drank heavily that night and slept on a park bench. Then, his footsteps refused to walk again on the way to that apartment.

Within a few months, he got divorced as he wished. Whether the wife was compelled or not, she readily accepted the divorce. However, all the expenses including the upbringing of the son for eighteen years old have to be borne by the father alone.

Everyone knew that he was now looking for a future wife. If not, how? Whoever he met would advertise himself after he got drunk.

Pasang opened his mouth like a child without any context. "A woman needs sex more than money! I don't have much property, but I have two wives. If I still get it, I think I should bring another wife. Can't you satisfy even one wife? Is there rust on your weapon?" In a drunken mood, he pointed his middle finger at the journalist.

Those who had been laughing, chatting, teasing, drinking and enjoying themselves were shocked as if a black man carrying a machine gun had just entered the room!

The journalist half-laughed and said, "You are like a goat left in the temple, chasing women! I am not like that. And I am not a macho-man like you. Well, you should be proud to be a macho-man! Yes, I am not a macho-man. I accept it!"

After the journalist displayed his weakness in front of everyone, who could ask another question? Pasang was speechless. Instead of asking another question, they all began to dig deeper

into themselves. Everyone was skeptical that a crisis like the one experienced by a journalist would apply to their own lives. In the United States, whatever happens in a relationship when a husband and wife earn the same amount!

Those who had a wife in the United States had to be so skeptical, what would be the mood of having a wife in Nepal! The issue of the journalist's family break-up raised questions and suspicions in the minds of everyone present at the restaurant.

Dhakal's heart shrank a little too much. His wife was in Nepal. He had not yet obtained a green card to take his wife to the United States. Even if he had doubts in his mind about his wife, he could not find any strong clues to confirm that his wife was having an affair with anyone. And he had no choice but to convince himself that his wife was good. In the Mahabharata, the Pandavas had no choice but to fight a war with the Kauravas!

Everyone was quietly involved in the accounting of their own lives for a while.

The colonel did not like to engage in personal gossip and debate. And he descended into introspection. Why do those who come to drink to have fun get into the personal life of others and laugh? If everything was perfect in Nepal, why would they come abroad to suffer? Everyone drinks alcohol with their own money, hardly anyone has come here in the hope of others. Everyone has their own earnings, more or less. Sharing tables with acquaintances makes the atmosphere of fun even denser!

Seeing that the atmosphere was very bad, the colonel teased Pasang to change the atmosphere, "Oh, Pasang! What is the idea of going to Nepal? Is the idea of living a retired life with the eldest wife dead or still alive?"

"I will leave after four years. At the same time, I will be sixty-five years old. I have paid

taxes for so many years. My allowance will be about twelve hundred dollars. With that much money, my old age will be spent happily in Nepal!" Pasang got excited. Suppose, the dream that has been in his mind for years is already dancing in front of his eyes!

"Would you survive four more years by drinking alcohol like this from morning till night? Will your dream of spending the rest of your life happily in Nepal come true? Have you ever thought about it? You are always drunk! Where is the time for you to think?" The journalist took revenge on Pasang in front of everyone, but he did not like Pasang's deep friendship with alcohol. No matter what Pasang said, he was a pure-hearted person! The journalist had his own internal evaluation.

The colonel did not find it appropriate to tease and ridicule one another. No intellectual debate, no discussion on contemporary issues! Who can digest more alcohol, who has flirted with another's wife, who has had an affair with so many women, whose wife has had an affair with someone, all these things have become more popular in such gatherings!

If there were only two or three people, they would listen to each other. In the hustle and bustle, who has time to listen to whom? Everyone starts chanting only their own 'raga'! The colonel did not think it appropriate to stay there. He shook hands with everyone and left.

The colonel thought to himself, *even if you don't turn over the book, you can learn and understand the knowledge in this Nepali kitchen.* He did not tell his grievances to others, but his mind would tell him from time to time!

As if he could not hear the sad melody of his heart, he started shortening the way home with his feet!

22

He had never dreamed that he would hear an unimaginable event in his lifetime. Let's say it's like something beyond a dream! You have to be ready to hear, see and experience something you never thought possible in life! The major's eyes of knowledge opened.

He received the news of the Durbar massacre one morning. Except for Prince Dipendra, the entire family, including the king and queen, was massacred! Dipendra was in a coma! He killed all the members of his family and shot himself in the end.

The news spread like a whirlwind of summer, moving from town to town, from village to village, from place to place, from children to the elderly.

At first, he did not believe the news. He thought it was April Fool's Day. What to do without believing, that was the real incident! The information came officially from the top level. And he found himself as if he had no guardian!

He speculated that the days to come would be like a man in a whirlpool. Now time will definitely not move at the same speed, it will stagger! His sixth sense spoke.

He remained alert as per the orders of the headquarters. He instructed his troops to remain alert, saying, "Anything can happen now. Be careful! No one should ask for leave immediately. When the situation changes, another order will come from above. No one should leave the barracks alone. Let me know if anyone leaves."

He saw a dark cloud of fear, terror, apprehension and curiosity hanging over everyone's face. Suppose there is going to be heavy rain at the same time, even with thunderstorms and hail!

The days went by in the same old routine. The CDO would come every evening with a bottle of whiskey, a gift to stay in the shelter and feel safe! Again, in the barracks, there was no shortage of snacks. He had also met a friend to drink and talk till midnight. Otherwise, where could he go to find other entertainment in that remote place!

From time to time at night, the Maoists would indiscriminately fire their guns from the hills, showing their presence. They were creating terror in the minds of the people. In response, firing from the police station also continued, demonstrating their presence.

The army watched the spectacle silently. It was an order from above, to be silent and alert. 'This is all a political battle, not a revolt against the state!' was the message conveyed to the army. Thinking left and right was like being banned in the army.

After consuming the salary and allowances of the state, the interest of the state was to be considered! The king's order became the first priority for the army. Then there was border security, the rescue of lives and property in natural disasters, the construction of roads in leisure, and the waiting to see when it would be their turn to join the peacekeeping force!

This was the routine of the army. They did not have to fight a war. They did not have to fight with internal power. They didn't even think that they would have to fight against external forces!

Even though he had not been home for months, he thought to himself. The memory of his family did not bother him much. He used to enjoy it outside the house. That is why his life philosophy was to get a job in the army.

But, from time to time, he felt bored with this barren place and his life like a prisoner! He did not have a reliable answer as to when he would be able to escape from here. Immediately he saw no way out. The patient, who had been receiving treatment at the hospital for a long time, was waiting impatiently for the doctor to discharge him and return home!

He had no choice but to obey the orders of the headquarters. There was no question of resigning from the job. He was yet to become a colonel! In such a mood, he continued to ride the two-wheeled cycle of life by compromising with time.

Sitting with the CDO from evening to midnight, drinking alcohol, listening to the repetitive firing of both sides at night, waking up from time to time to hear the CDO roaring loudly while sleeping soundly, this was his daily routine! And one more thing waiting for the postman to bring the transfer letter was added to his daily routine!

He was also realizing that new scenarios were being staged in the country day by day. To understand this, he did not have to be a student of political science!

Time is not moving in the right direction. The time clock can ring the alarm at any time! His six senses awoke again.

23

He was sleeping under the influence of alcohol. The soldier woke him up in the middle of the night and said, "Sir! Someone has called you. He should talk to you! It's urgent!"

Who called to tell the news at midnight? He could not guess. Certainly not from home? It must be an official thing! He predicted.

He picked up the receiver. When he was about to say 'hello', he received a message from the other side, "Be very careful! The Maoists have attacked the Dang barracks and looted a lot of weapons and ammunition. Many of our soldiers have been killed. All the information is not available now, we will know by tomorrow."

He received instructions and information from the head office. Suddenly, he felt dizzy.

The timing is not right. Now the road will definitely not be like walking on the highway, it will be like walking on the narrow road made by cutting down the hill! His conscience spoke.

He did not think it appropriate to wake everyone up in the middle of the night to report the incident. He lay down on the bed thinking that they should be briefed tomorrow. Sleep also escaped his eyes. In his mind, the war of thoughts began. Now it seems that the time has come to fight! His mind said. He made up his mind. Such terrorists must be eliminated now, he decided in his heart.

Before he said it, everyone had heard about the incident on radio and TV. All that was left for them to do was to receive instructions from Major Saab on what to do next. Mentally, everyone was alert. They were not ready for war from their internal hearts. Along with their job duties, the torment inflicted by the state was now mixed with responsibility.

The government immediately declared a state of emergency. Soon the troops came out of the closed barracks and suddenly gathered in the open field. Suppose a storm brings dust and dirt from four directions and piles it up in one place!

An emergency order was issued to increase patrolling in villages, cities and forests. He also asked to strengthen the barracks, bunkers and sentries to make the barracks safe. And he instructed everyone to sleep a lot during the day and stay awake at night. He assigned the captain the task of sending different soldiers to patrol different places every day.

He exhorted the junior officers and soldiers to carry out their responsibilities properly, saying, "The war is not won by fighting alone, the whole team must fight honestly. And then it wins. War is like a football game. We need the full support of the entire team." He gave a short speech.

Unexpected moments in life are bound to come, without any prior notice! Coming secretly! When he went to work in the army, where did he imagine such a day? If I had imagined that such a day would come, I would have been willing to enter the flames on purpose! He doubted himself.

Today, he missed his family very much. The whole family was worried about him. Although he told his family on the phone that there was no need to worry, there was no question that the family would not worry because of the bad things happening in the country day by day. Everyone was worried.

The general public feared that anyone who dared to attack the barracks and loot weapons could do anything. However, this does not mean that the soldiers who were ready for war did not feel fear and terror! Again, being an Army Major does not mean that he had no fear in his mind!

The day was easy for everyone in the barracks. However, the question of whether the Maoists would come to attack at night would have taken root in everyone's mind. The bullets

raining down from the hill towards the police post were now falling towards the barracks. Well, even if it did not cause any physical damage, the psychological effect on the soldiers was unbearable!

Staying up late at night, keeping the soldiers on duty drunk, sleeping in the wee hours of the morning, getting up in the middle of the day, getting ready for battle all the time, patrolling the village in the afternoon had become a regular routine of the army.

It was the duty of the army to look at the passers-by with suspicion, to search, to intimidate, to slap, to detain and torture them for interrogation. The obligation to get paid had to be fulfilled anyway!

The colonel woke up early in the morning. He was lying on the bed. His wife was still fast asleep. And in his mind, many things started talking to each other.

He did not want to live in the United States at all. However, his wife refused to return to Nepal and always said, "Even though I can't earn a living by working, I live here with my son and daughter even if I take care of their children. If I did that, they would take care of me happily!"

He was upset to see his wife's fascination with America. At times, he even thought of going to Nepal secretly without letting his wife know. But he could not dare from within his mind.

"What are you going to do there alone?" His mind would suddenly ask him a question.

He was unresponsive, as if he could not answer the question he did not understand! And his passion for going to Nepal was slowing down, as if the hot rice had cooled down in a few minutes in the winter months!

His enjoyment in the army and his intimate relationship with women did not go unnoticed by his wife. Even if his wife did not see it with her own eyes, she would have believed the words of those who saw it.

"Don't trust the army!" Relatives and well-wishers used to harass his wife from time to time. While being a wife at home, the stories of soldiers keeping girls secretly outside also became a talk of women spending time in their spare time. Why would his wife be absent in such an environment?

There was nothing to follow the gossip until she saw it with her own eyes and said it with her husband's mouth. She kept such doubts in her mind, thinking that she would bear the burden herself, but she did not allow such rumors to reach her ears. 'Whatever happens, I will endure!' She used to make her mind strong.

Even in the United States, sometimes the argument seems to be invincible, but his wife would beat him up by exposing his past deeds. He used to keep quiet for fear that his wife would expose him by digging into the past. Instead, he looked like a withered flower!

His silence was considered by his wife as her victory. In this way, their mutual quarrels and disputes would be settled by reaching a tacit agreement and understanding. Both were in a win-win situation. Both of them did not accept defeat, they considered themselves victorious.

Even though his body was lying on the same bed with his wife now, his mind was somewhere! The mind was free, it was cool! The mind did not have to wait for anyone's order on where to walk, where to climb, where to rest!

Whenever his mind was eager to return to Nepal, it was as if the eyes of the new bride were repeatedly fixed on the courtyard to see if anyone had come to pick her up from her family!

You have to endure many things in life, whether you want to or not! The word 'compulsion' is the most important. Your desire doesn't make much sense! Where is life under your control? Just as a showman makes a monkey dance at his beck and call, so time does not dance at his beck and call!

He took a deep breath. He had never imagined that he would come to America and stay here for a long time.

"What are you thinking? You're thinking about going to Nepal again, aren't you? What's on your mind? What's in Nepal? Who's in

Nepal? We're all here. Are you haunted by the memory of an old girl-friend?" His wife was furious.

He did not know when his wife woke up. He didn't say anything. To speak at such a time was like adding kerosene to a burning fire. He had grown up in the habit of listening to his wife's murmurs in silence, but not replying. After a while, he thought that his wife would get tired and keep quiet. He thought that the fire of the stove should not be burnt on the roof of the house in anger!

After spending twenty-five years together, there was no question of not knowing each other's shortcomings. Leaving aside each other's strengths, we are also becoming accustomed to vices. Though the thinking is different, the thread that connects the mind is different. The moment of sorrow is more tied to each other than the moment of happiness! The thread of a knotted relationship cannot be untied easily! The colonel thought to himself.

The question of how to live as a third-class citizen in another's country sometimes spreads like wildfire in his mind.

He wanted to live the rest of his life according to his own will, he had not inculcated any sin in his mind. However, he could not persuade his wife to return to Nepal!

Does life mean just following the rhythm of time or guiding your mind? He asked himself. But he did not get a satisfactory answer.

Perhaps, there was still a long way to go for the answer, he thought. And even after taking a long time, he calmed the agitated mind for a few days.

25

It was not a new thing for the countrymen to hear and see the incidents of terror, murder, abduction, disappearance, annihilation, rape, attack, explosion, clash, ambush etc. on a daily basis. How could the people walk freely during the day and sleep soundly at night when the country itself was going through a state of transition!

In the end, the general public had to suffer, whether from the state or the rebels. It was as if the smile from the lips of the people went underground! It was as if fear, dread, terror, doubt, apprehension were holding everyone tightly!

Troops had been ordered by the state to be deployed in villages, towns, markets, roads, squares, highways, streets, alleys, forests, jungles, everywhere. At night it was a responsibility to protect the barracks, but during the day it was free for them, they had their own law and order!

They did not have to wait for the above order to search anyone they met on the way, detain them on suspicion of being Maoists or eliminate them in the name of encounter. What their conscience thought was like the final order!

Ambushing, kidnapping and killing of unarmed police on leave, killing of civilians in the name of enemy intelligence, physical damage and physical torture on the pretext of non-payment of donations were all part of the Maoist policy.

The general public was the victim of both sides!

Major Rajendra Khadka used to incite the soldiers from time to time, "These terrorists are traitors. They must be killed. Don't be afraid. We have to go out on our own to confront them. Don't wait for them to come to attack the barracks, you know?"

He used to go on patrol commanding himself. Major Khagendra Rai, a close friend of his from the same batch, was abducted by the Maoists on his way home. And brutally tortured and killed by a khukuri. That incident aroused in him a great deal of resentment and revenge against the Maoists.

From time to time, the Maoists would declare a Nepal Bandh. Vehicles would stop. Merchants were afraid to open shops. He would try to open the market with some soldiers. He used to show guns and frighten the traders to open shops.

He used to threaten those who refused to open the shop, "You must be a supporter of the Maoists. You help them by donating. I will take you into custody on this pretext. Then the day may come when your family will have to search for your name on the missing persons list!"

What could the shopkeepers do? If the shops were opened, the shopkeepers would be targeted by the Maoists, if not, they would be accused of supporting the Maoists. The major's dreadful threat was to withstand them. His ruthless behavior caused a great deal of panic among those involved in the trade and business, and a small amount of enthusiasm among the general public, and added to the resentment of the rebels.

He became popular in the district due to such activities. He had earned more enemies than friends. He didn't care! He had every right to use his power without having to wait for orders from above. All he had to do was exercise his discretion properly!

He was being discussed in the local newspapers. An underground newspaper dedicated to the Maoists reported threats to attack the barracks. He used to laugh at such things, "Come here to attack. What will happen to them? Even their main leader will bite his tongue!"

Even though he said this, his mind was not impatient waiting for war! He wished that the

whirlpool of war would not enter his barracks as much as possible! Who doesn't love life? A person who always thinks of suicide is different!

"Tonight, at the house of a Maoist leader, his daughter's wedding is taking place. I have learned from insiders that most of the Maoist leaders and activists in the district will also be present." A reliable informant informed him secretly.

This is a great opportunity for a Maoist operation, such an opportunity does not come often! He thought. The greed to become a colonel grew in him. A thousand watts of light shone in his eyes. He informed the general, who was in touch with him at the headquarters, over the phone and asked for instructions on what to do. And the general hung up the phone saying he would answer in an hour.

An hour later, the general said in command language, "Don't give up! Attack with full readiness. I'm sure you'll do well. It doesn't matter if there are some casualties during the operation. Such is the fate of those who support such traitorous terrorists! Don't be afraid, I am with you. If you take action well, you will be covered in the media. Also, it will be easier for me to recommend you for a promotion."

Why did he back down after getting so much support from the General? He remembered the face of his friend who had been brutally killed by the Maoists. The moments spent with him flashed in his eyes. Because of his revenge, the blood in his veins started running a hundred meters instead of a marathon!

He chose soldiers who were especially fearless in the barracks, ready to fight, and who hated the Maoists completely. And he announced his plan. He kept the rest of the army guarding the barracks.

"If the information received is not correct and if there is deception, on the contrary, they can attack the barracks!" The training he received in the army, the knowledge he gained while joining the peace-keeping force and his own conscience also alerted him.

After dinner, the soldiers led by Major began to climb the hill. The wedding house was in a remote village. It was not difficult for them to climb the hill as they drank alcohol. Instead, they proceeded to take precautions to avoid being ambushed. They didn't have to think twice that the wedding house was the same when they saw the lights burning in the dark from a distance.

Of course, there are many Maoists. They may have come fully armed. Action should be taken carefully, not in a hurry! The major's intuition alerted him.

He first ordered the soldiers to surround the wedding house. He observed from a distance the activities of the Maoists and the number of armed men. Now, he thought for a moment about miking or attacking directly. Again, the general public may have been involved in the marriage, why risk their lives! The hard ice that had frozen in his heart melted a little.

And before the attack, the major miked urging the Maoists to surrender, "You are all under our siege. Surrender with all your weapons! We order the old men and children to leave now, but only after checking. We capture the young and the middle-aged. We will take them and release them after interrogation and investigation. This is the final order. Surrender soon, or we will open fire in no time!"

The hustle and bustle that used to be in the wedding house had now turned into silence. Suppose a fierce storm entered a squatter settlement and blew off the roofs of all the squatters' houses and suddenly calmed down!

There was no response from the marriage house. Maybe they were discussing with each other, he guessed. After a while, the firing started from the wedding house. The reaction of action

is the law of nature! In response, he ordered the soldiers to open fire.

There was heavy firing from both sides. The general public ran away and cried. Now a common question arose in the minds of the soldiers as to who should be stopped, who should be captured and who should be targeted.

Everyone even has to practice the religion of saving one's own life before taking the life of others! It is the universal rule of war not to shoot the unarmed as much as possible and to shoot even if the armed ones are chased away!

The double firing continued for several hours. The major did not even have time to think about how many casualties there were, how many lives were lost, how many were injured, how much damage was done to the army. The Maoists had to be defeated anyway. The war was to be won by killing them as much as possible, or by injuring them severely! And in the end, even if the army could not win, the rebels had to be arrested anyway! There was no turning back, hiding the tail like a dog!

After three or four hours of fighting, perhaps with many casualties, the Maoists raised the issue of surrender. They dropped their weapons and went out, raising their hands. The armies took control of them all. The soldiers tied their hands behind their backs. And everyone was lined up to walk.

Some soldiers on the army side were also wounded, they were put on stretchers. Leaving the dead and severely wounded of the Maoists in the care of the villagers, the troops set off.

What to do with these Maoist terrorists who were captured alive and surrendered? A question arose in the major's mind. As the soldiers were severely wounded and the Maoists opened fire instead of surrendering at the beginning, hatred was firmly planted in the major's mind.

Even the prisoners were walking on the path of the forest with fear in their eyes, apprehension as well as a little persuasion and humility.

Knowing that General was fast asleep, the major called General's house from the walkie-talkie. He told the general all the details of the incident and asked the general for advice on what to do with the captured Maoists.

The general gave the same order, which his mind had already thought.

In the middle of the forest, he ordered all the prisoners to line up. He ordered everyone to lie down on the ground. One of them was a pregnant woman, probably with a five-month-old baby in her womb! She grabbed the major's leg and cried out not to kill her for the sake of the baby. However, the major's heart did not melt like snow, but hardened like a rock.

Everyone looked as helpless as a goat to be sacrificed. Death stood before their eyes!

"Melting like butter in someone's tears is like a warrior who accepts defeat even after winning a war!" His conscience awoke.

He did not want to waste time thinking about unnecessary things. Instead, he let the greed for promotion grow in his mind, like a wild mushroom growing in the rainy season! He used to slaughter goats all over the village during the festivals. Pressing the trigger of a gun was a very easy game for him!

After a while, all the prisoners fell to the ground and calmed down. Leaving all the previous fears, anxieties, apprehensions, crying, persuasion, humility, and all the dreams they had cherished in their hearts, they walked the path of another world, promising never to return!

The money was well earned. Now I have to park the car and go to Jackson Heights, he thought. He did not need to go anywhere else. He must have known the streets of New York, because his job was to drive!

He wanted to flee to Nepal because of the same skyscrapers in New York, the rush of cars, the huge crowd of people. He wanted to enjoy the quiet lap of nature away from the dazzling world!

What to do only when you want and when the situation is hostile! He took care of himself. What else could he do but wait for the situation to come to him one day?

After parking the car, he walked straight to the Nepali kitchen. After buying whiskey as usual, he entered the Nepali kitchen. And he looked around. He saw Hamal drinking alone on the corner table. And sitting in the chair next to the table where Hamal was sitting, he said, "I feel like you have a good income today. I never saw you come here before nine o'clock!"

"Your wife earns money and so does your daughter, but ours doesn't! I have to take care of my young children by paying house rent, car installment and insurance on my own income! They don't want to work. The daughter sometimes goes to work, but in two days she leaves saying she doesn't like it. The son doesn't do that much.

My son doesn't speak well to me. What's on his mind, I haven't figured out yet. Sometimes it feels like I made a mistake by taking them to America!"

Hamal expressed his family's grief.

"Today's children are like that, they have no responsibility. Parents have taken care of everything. As they get older, they will begin to understand the responsibility! Well, now let's hand over all these complaints to time and let's have a fun conversation. Why bother worrying about your children right now? When the time comes, they will carry the burden of their own worries!" the colonel turned the matter around.

He wondered why we should make the pleasant atmosphere unpleasant by telling others about our sorrows and problems that we have to carry for the rest of our lives.

The colonel was well aware of Hamal's problem. Hamal's problem was the exact opposite of his problem! Hamal did not want to go to Nepal, his wife did not want to come to the United States to work. The money from renting a house in Nepal would have been enough to support his wife's lonely life. The children also came here after getting Hamal's green card, carrying the American Dream!

If he sent his wife two or three hundred dollars a month, he would not have to listen to her. Even if his wife was not with him, in his wife's memory, if he had spent more than two hours at work to spend an hour with a Mexican girl, it would have been enough!

Even if he was not with his wife, his life would go on like a kingdom without a king!

Before they could say cheers, then suddenly appeared a weird person, Pasa!

The colonel did not even know the real name of Pasa. The colonel knew that he was the son of a Newari father and a Tibetan mother. Pasa does not share his story with anyone. No one knows what is on his mind. The colonel never really believed Pasa. Pasa always comes here hoping that someone will give him alcohol, but the colonel doesn't remember that he ever came with alcohol!

"Come on, let's sit down," the colonel called to Pasa. That's all I have to say to a man I know, the colonel thought. He drinks a little alcohol, what a waste! The colonel spoke to himself.

In the United States, for alcohol, you don't even have to set aside money from your household budget. You don't even have to cut back on anything you need to buy alcohol. Only, you have to take care of your health! That's what your family says.

Knowing that Hamal did not like Pasa, he settled Pasa together. Asking for a glass, he poured whiskey. As soon as Pasa saw the whiskey, the colonel smiled when he saw a different kind of happiness on Pasa's face.

Pasa's problem was also of its own kind. He was alone. He used to live with his daughter and son-in-law. What's more, he has stopped living with his daughter and son-in-law and is now sharing a room with someone. Even at the age of fifty-nine, he does night duty as a security guard four days a week. It has been two years since he said that his wife would come in two months, but why, his wife has not come yet. If you ask him, he has not stopped saying that his wife is coming now!

Pasa never tells the truth, only he knows or God!

Colonel, Hamal and Pasa all drank comfortably and emptied their bottles. They stopped talking for a while. They didn't have anything new to talk about. Pasa had more to do with drinking than talking. When the whiskey ran out, they gave him money to buy another bottle, he was always ready to run to the store anytime!

Since Colonel and Hamal run Uber, there was a lot of talk between them about that! Same parking problem! Complaint about the police giving tickets directly even for a small mistake! Not being able to eat on time! One day you will earn well, the next day you will not earn at all! Instead of going to the toilet to urinate after drinking a lot of water, it is better to soak your throat with a little water! A similar conversation took place between them.

From time to time, except for running to the liquor store, Pasa remained silent. He didn't pay attention to them, just pretended to listen. Instead, he got lost in his own world drinking alcohol, like a meditative saint who can't be distracted by the crowd and noise of thousands of people!

28

Terror, kidnappings, murders, explosions and clashes were taking place all over the country every day. Time was running out between the state security forces and the rebels to figure out how to kill each other. From time to time, the game of ceasefire was going on in the name of negotiations!

Yes, only when there was a ceasefire did he get a chance to go home! Even when going home, the army had to be very careful! Moreover, he was popular in the eyes of the people in the district and a great enemy in the eyes of the Maoists. He must be alert.

On his way home and back, he often waited for a helicopter to come, overseeing the district and carrying supplies. He did not use an army vehicle for fear of being ambushed. And traveling in public transport, there was a possibility of being abducted by the Maoists.

Again, the Maoists could break the ceasefire at any time. The Maoists, like the astrologers, should not have seen an auspicious time to declare war by attacking a police post or barracks!

Days, months, years went by without asking anyone. The transfer letter from the headquarters was like a lost passenger, he had not got a chance to see it!

After living in the same place for years, he also felt very bored. In any case, he could not bear the great tragedy that his friends endured. Some of his batch members lost their lives, some were ambushed and maimed, some were abducted on the way home on holiday and lost their lives. In this case, he was lucky!

"Military people should always be alert, whether waking up or sleeping!" He used to chant like a mantra. And he also advised the soldiers to chant the mantra.

In a short time, the seven parties and the Maoists intensified the street agitation by reaching a twelve-point agreement. And within a few days, the king's government was forced to bow before the people. Eventually, the king was forced to hand over power to the protesters.

And he was also transferred to the headquarters. He was promoted to colonel by adding a medal to his uniform. He was relieved that his work was appreciated. He saluted the General from the bottom of his heart for fulfilling his promise!

Even in the city, he felt that his life would not be easy. He did not see the comfort of living at home. Maoist leaders and cadres seemed to cover villages, cities and even the capital!

He thought that whoever he saw was a Maoist. He wondered if the man had known him. He was trying to remember if he was from the same district where he was posted. He wondered if he had killed any of his family members!

He had only fear and doubt in his mind and he didn't have to ask his brain what to do now to spend time when he didn't have any responsibility other than to show up at the office. His feet automatically went straight to the shelter of alcohol!

Alcohol greeted him with an open heart. Drinking alcohol no longer had to do with sunset or sunrise for him! Simply, his soul had to ask for alcohol!

During the day, security guards would accompany him wherever he went, there was nothing to be afraid of. At night he was alone. While sleeping at home, he used to sleep with his father's rifle under his head. Because, during the conflict, he had made so many enemies!

He was always aware that the enemy could take revenge at any time. He seldom slept at home. Sometimes he would go to a relative's place to take shelter, sometimes he would go to a friend's house carrying a bottle of liquor. He didn't stay anywhere for many days, he kept moving like a cat!

He wondered if someone was really spying on him! He himself was confused. Seeing the way to enter the tunnel, someone entered, but he was confused as he could not find the way out!

When the ray of hope in his mind was covered with a thick blanket of despair, he would drown in alcohol.

Fear and terror reigned in his mind. There was no question that he liked the new environment and atmosphere, but he was starting to feel bitter as if he was chewing bitter gourd raw. In the old environment, the dignity, honor, respect and pride he had got was trampled by the strong feet of the time. He was very sad and disgusted with the present.

He had no regrets about what he had done in the past. He was taught that a citizen who has vowed to serve the state must fulfill his duty and that the main thing is to win the war, even if it is by deception!

He no longer felt safe inside the country. He had seen increasing Maoist interference everywhere. And again, who would guarantee that he would not be targeted any day, neither the state nor the rebels!

It was better to make concrete decisions in life than to live helplessly like a parakeet. And he met the same general and asked him to send him to the US for training. The general was also aware of his problem. With the help of the general, he and his wife also got visas. According to the advice, they planned to leave their children at home and fly to America.

There was no question that his wife was unhappy! She had to get a chance to meet her husband here. In any case, she was happy that her husband would always be with her in the United States.

After arriving in the United States, he applied for asylum on the advice of a lawyer. Due to his job position and the news published in the newspaper, his file was approved within six months. After getting the green card, their children also came to the United States. And in America, everything had settled down.

It was not his desire to come to America, it was his obligation!

He would sometimes ask himself, "Would I have been a driver in the United States if the Maoists had not started an armed war?"

The answer, as always, was silence.

And he would yell at himself, "Fuck! Our life is like a dice! We have to run on the player! Wherever the player throws, we have to fall! There is nothing under our control!"

Suppose, after coming to America, he got divine vision. And without any hesitation or complaint in his mind, he quietly followed the steps of time. Reckless!

The colonel was drinking alone in the Nepali kitchen today. Even though they were acquaintances, he did not see anyone who could get along and drink together.

He doesn't share his thoughts with anyone, but he has a habit of listening to others. He thought that he would know what he was saying and that he would get new information by listening to what others said.

Listening to others, I should drink alcohol comfortably now, the colonel thought.

Everyone has their own story. It's as if the story of one doesn't exactly match with the other, as if one's face doesn't match with the other at all! The twins are an exception!

He did not see much activity in the Nepali kitchen today. Most of the people who were there, probably hungry, were eating the same Nepali food. Suppose, a cow that had been tied up for two days without food was taken to a newly-grown cornfield and left loose!

Some of them were kneeling on their mobile phones. It was as if he had no time to talk to a friend sitting at the same table! Something less than a handful has taken over the world! He thought deeply. Religion ruled in Dwapara Yuga while technology ruled in Kali Yuga!

He did not turn his eyes and mind to others, but returned to his own life. It was as if a drunken man saw a traffic check and made a U-turn!

It has been eleven or twelve years since I entered the United States. How fast time passed! He meditated. The first year he came to the United States, he felt like he was in prison! It was a matter of thousands of miles beyond his imagination to come here and do something he had never done in his life!

The last few years had been a little easier for him. He got used to it. He was mingling in this environment. Just like those who have spent their lives in prison are slowly getting used to enjoying the atmosphere inside the prison!

The desire to return to Nepal and live happily in a beautiful village for the rest of his life would rain down in his mind from time to time.

But his desire was always hindered by the same sentence that his wife always used to say, "I will not return even if I die. What is there in Nepal? Here we have our whole family! Even the children do not want to go to Nepal. What can they do there? No! Whatever you do, whatever you want! I have nothing to say!"

He would suddenly become silent at the thought of 'what should I do when I go to Nepal alone in my old age'. Like a silent monk!

The issue of returning to Nepal has not been raised in front of his wife for a long time! He remembered immediately.

The crowd at the restaurant began to grow. The night was getting darker too. He thought that he had forgotten to look at the clock and was immersed in imagination! He pushed the boat of thought to the shore and turned his ear towards the noise.

"I am very lucky. I got a job in the United States after getting a DV. I earn more money here in three weeks than I used to earn in a year by teaching in Nepal, man!" One was proud.

"I came to America after crossing the river. I paid off my debts in three or four years. Now I can save my earnings! But sometimes, when I am tormented by the memory of my wife and son, I feel like carrying a suitcase and walking now! I am satisfied that I was finally able to enter the United States with so many expenses and risks in my life. I have spent so many years thinking that I will win the case from the court and bring my wife and son here. But when will the dream come

true?"Another expressed his grief.

The ring of the mobile distracted him. The word 'wife' appeared on the screen of his mobile. He touched OK.

"Where are you? It's ten o'clock! I saw the car in the parking lot near our house. You must be in the same Nepali kitchen. It's been an hour since I came home. What's wrong when you come home early? Just sit with your friends and drink alcohol. You don't give us time!"

Instead of listening to his wife's long murmur, he hung up the phone.

The road was not deserted, but there was little movement of vehicles and people.

Alone, on top of that, shaking a little on the side of the road under the influence of alcohol, silently communicating with the mind, whispering melodious melodies in the deep emptiness of the night, even returning to one's home like a bird, has a different taste in the pleasures of life! Well, even those who don't taste it are considered vain!

Today I will revive the issue of returning to Nepal with my wife, he decided. I cheat on my wife a lot and even threaten her a little!

He rehearsed the dialogue that he would tell his wife at home, "How long will we live just for the sake of our children? Tomorrow they will have their own family. They want freedom, everyone wants their own space! At such times, everyone starts to feel lonely from the person they love so much. Then, one's own life begins to burden oneself! It is the spouse who is needed and supportive in such a situation!"

This dialogue might not have much effect on his wife today, but he was sure that it would play a decisive role in the near future.

How did Krishna force Arjuna, who did not want to fight the war by throwing the bow on the ground, to carry the bow again with the help of words! That is why it is said that 'words are more effective than weapons!'

"How long will my wife escape from the trap of my words like a watchful fish, one day she will fall into my trap!" He laughed heartily.

Imagining the plan of his life to go to Nepal, he lost himself again in his own magical world, like a meditative yogi sitting in Nirvana!